"Hey, what do you doing?"

"Looking at your driver's licence." Lucian raised it out of her reach, but JoJo went for it...and found herself against him. He was as solid as a rock... and warm. Beneath sleep-mussed hair, he looked dangerous. Her breath caught in her throat and she retreated.

"JoJo Weston. Five seven. Hundred and twenty-four pounds." He checked her to be certain.

"Satisfied? Now maybe you better show me *your* licence."

His grin was wolfish. "You're free to look for one."

He raised his arms, inviting her to search him. But the thought of touching him sent a rush of confusion through her.

"Maybe you'd like to check out my bedroom instead?" he said.

Dear Reader:

We are delighted to bring you this daring series from Silhouette®.

Intrigue™—where resourceful, beautiful women flirt with danger and risk everything for irresistible, often treacherous men.

Intrigue—where the stories are full of heart-stopping suspense and mystery lurks around every corner.

You won't be able to resist Intrigue's exciting mix of danger, deception... and desire.

Please write and let us know what you think of our selection of Intrigue novels. We'd like to hear from you.

Jane Nicholls
Silhouette Books
PO Box 236
Thornton Road
Croydon
Surrey
CR9 3RU

Lucky Devil

PATRICIA ROSEMOOR

▼™ SILHOUETTE

Intrigue™

*Silhouette and Colophon are registered trademarks of
Harlequin Books S.A., used under licence.*

*First published in Great Britain 1996
Silhouette Books, Eton House, 18-24 Paradise Road,
Richmond, Surrey TW9 1SR*

© Patricia Pinianski 1996

ISBN 0 373 22361 7

46-9610

*Printed and bound in Great Britain
by Mackays of Chatham PLC, Chatham*

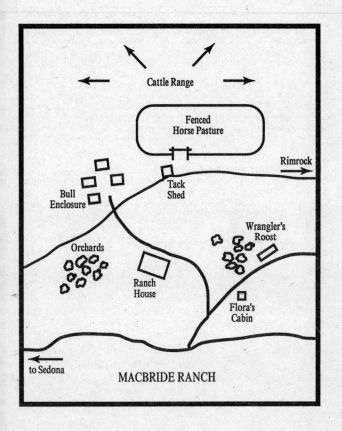

Cattle Range

Fenced
Horse Pasture

Rimrock

Bull
Enclosure

Tack
Shed

Wrangler's
Roost

Orchards

Ranch
House

Flora's
Cabin

to Sedona

MACBRIDE RANCH

To Linda Sweeny—for her usual "bull".

Prologue

Newspaper clippings spread across the scarred coffee table of the dingy motel room revealed nothing new, nothing to grasp on to. So far, they had given up no solid ideas on how to proceed. But they had to, given time. Yet there was none to waste, for time was of the essence.

Concentrate!

Maybe if arranged in a different order... A little shuffling of the lurid headlines wouldn't hurt. The tattered clippings moved around, replayed like a deck of cards until they came up with a winning hand.

There. That was better.

Vanished Show Girl Held Hostage... Bride-To-Be's Experience No *Honeymoon In Vegas*... Maintenance Man "Protects" Beloved... Dancer Hidden Below Showroom... Show Girl Released After Week's Ordeal.

The headlines, now in logical order, told *her* side of the story.

The accompanying photographs told yet another lie.

The slender woman staring out of the grainy photos appeared ragged, raw, emotionally drained. Her face was too pale, a splash of freckles—the curse of natural redheads—prominent across her nose. Her wide mouth was parted, not in a smile, but as if she were trying to suck in air. Her eyes were dark pools of pain.

All in all, she personified innocence unfairly assaulted.

An act. A ploy for sympathy.

She was good at that, eliciting compassion from the unsuspecting. From men especially. Did this come naturally to her? Or had she developed the talent in classes as she had her dancing? Maybe she should have been an actress. She'd fooled a lot of people. But not everyone.

Some recognized the truth.

JoJo Weston was a slippery sort, a tarnished gypsy who had gotten only part of what was coming to her. Unfortunately, she'd escaped her fate with the help of her loyal friends. Too bad for her. Better had she never risen from her dungeon. Better had she died there. Then she wouldn't present such a problem.

A temporary situation.

JoJo Weston had no idea of what was in store for her. She thought she'd had a scary experience before; she was in for one hell of a roller coaster ride now.

With some determined help, fate was about to take another shot at her . . . and this time, she wouldn't escape.

Chapter One

Flying out of the Caribbean, JoJo Weston ran as if the hounds of hell were on her heels. She could have taken one of the limos, but the traffic on the Strip was at its peak. Running along the tourist-packed sidewalks was faster, even in heels.

Only two blocks to the Fantasy Wedding Chapel, where her unsuspecting best friend was about to marry the man she loved—unsuspecting that the maid of honor had forgotten the groom's ring, that is, and had returned to the hotel long enough to fetch the thick gold band. JoJo now wore the ring on her thumb, where she couldn't misplace it.

A red light stopped her in her tracks. Taking a deep, slow breath, she looked around at the other people piling up at the corner to cross the street.

That's when she saw the figure lurking behind a couple of brawny college-age guys slightly behind and to her right. JoJo started at that bony frame, those glasses that bobbled on the too-small nose. Then the image was swallowed by the crowd now shoving her forward.

The light had changed.

Heart pounding wildly, JoJo stumbled off the curb. A middle-aged man in plaid shorts and a garish Las Vegas T-shirt grabbed her upper arm and saved her from a fall.

"You all right, miss?"

"Yes, thank you."

But she wasn't all right. Might never be again.

JoJo forced herself to move, her legs carrying her across the street in slow motion. Every step was an effort. She felt overheated, slightly dizzy and filled with a familiar and growing dread. Though she kept checking the crowd around and behind her, she didn't see anything ominous.

And yet the threat wouldn't subside.

Nearly every hour of every day, JoJo was uncomfortable in her own skin. Often, the sensation of someone following her, watching her, made the hair at the back of her neck stand up. She knew it was because of what had happened to her—she was experiencing some kind of delayed shock syndrome that had yet to play itself out. Even knowing that, her imagination wouldn't rest. For the past few weeks, she'd been looking over her shoulder wherever she went.

But she had never before thought she'd seen Lester Perkins, who she knew was locked up in a psycho ward at the county jail, awaiting trial.

Several cars now sat outside the Fantasy Wedding Chapel, including the '68 Corvette Mako Shark that belonged to the groom, and a more sedate if equally expensive limousine that belonged to his father. JoJo knew the handful of invited guests who could come had arrived.

Unfortunately, Sasha's parents had been forced to cancel flying in from New York when her dad broke his leg. And one of Sasha's sisters was ready to go into labor at any moment and needed the third sister to supervise her kids. Everyone had been disappointed, but Nick would send Sasha's family a video of the wedding and fly them all into Las Vegas later for a family celebration.

Entering the air-conditioned chapel, JoJo tucked away the fear that she was teetering on the edge of a nervous breakdown. This was her best friend's wedding, for heaven's sake, a day to be happy. She almost ran into the groom, dressed in a tropical white silk-blend suit and yellow-and-purple flower-printed silk shirt, a fancier version of what she thought of as his hotel uniform. Nick Donatelli, the owner of the Caribbean, was both her boss and her friend.

"Sasha's been looking for you," he said, nervously pulling a hand through his dark hair. "Hey, you okay?"

"Yeah, just out of breath," she assured him, unused to seeing Nick looking unsure of himself. "I'll go find her right away."

She felt his intent green gaze follow as she made her way down the hall to the bride's room, where Sasha Brozynski was worriedly poking at her tawny tresses.

"Stop fussing or you'll ruin it," JoJo chided in the most natural tone she could muster.

"There you are!" Swinging around in her seat, Sasha widened her amber eyes at the sight before her. "What happened to you?"

JoJo caught a glance at her own disheveled appearance in the mirror. "Oh, no," she groaned.

Her naturally curly hair had frizzed. The brilliant yellow silk, fashioned into a flowing, loose halter-top gown was damp beneath her arms and around her breasts. Her makeup had simply melted in the June desert heat.

"You look like you ran a marathon."

JoJo lifted her thumb. "I had to go back to the hotel for this. In our rush to leave for the chapel, I left Nick's ring in your room."

Sasha rose, her lush six-foot frame accentuated by her unusual wedding gown—a silk sarong fashioned from the same yellow-and-purple material as Nick's shirt. "Sit," she commanded.

JoJo slipped into a chair before the mirrored wall, and Sasha attacked her frizzy hair with a curling iron, saying, "You'll be good as new in no time." When JoJo didn't respond, Sasha frowned at her through the mirror. "You are all right?"

Not wanting to put a damper on her friend's wedding day, JoJo thought to lie. And she would have if the fear chasing her had remained vague and at a safe distance. But her brush with the recent past had been too close for her nerves. She had no one else to tell who would understand.

"I thought I saw him."

"Who?"

"Lester."

"That's impossible."

"I know." A fluttery sensation in the pit of her stomach made JoJo shudder. "But I swear he really was there in the crowd for a moment before he disappeared."

"It's guilt," Sasha proposed. "We promised to visit him and haven't come through."

At the advice of Nick's lawyer, who felt they should distance themselves, at least until after the trial.

Sasha went on. "You saw someone who reminded you of Lester, is all."

"I suppose you're right."

"You got to stop focusing on it. Stop being victimized by a man who can't hurt you anymore."

"Lester never wanted to hurt me."

Secretly in love with JoJo, the mousy maintenance man had sworn to protect her from her own fiancé, who had turned out to be somebody else. Somebody dangerous. A murderer. In some part, she owed Lester.

"Yeah, but Lester did hurt you, if not physically, then in spirit," Sasha said.

Knowing her friend was right, JoJo sighed. "I keep seeing shadows where there are none," she admitted. "I think I need some time off."

"I tried to tell you." Sasha put the finishing touches on JoJo's red curls and fluffed them out with her long, brightly painted nails. "You don't just get over something like this instantly. I should know. You need time off *away* from Las Vegas."

Directly after being released from her temporary prison, JoJo had returned to work as if nothing had happened. She'd figured dancing was the best medicine, and for a few weeks, she'd been fine. Then the memories and her imagination had gotten hold of her. Oh, she was still able to forget for a few hours at a time, during her performances. Trouble was, there were twenty-four hours in a day.

"Maybe I should take a short vacation," JoJo admitted. "A few days away from everything familiar would do me good."

"A few weeks would be even better. Nicky will understand. I'll talk to him."

"When you get back from your honeymoon will be soon enough."

Fixing her makeup, JoJo took heart in the idea of getting away. A rest cure should do the trick, get her back on track. Only when she felt centered again could she get on with her life. Only then could she figure out what she wanted to do with the rest of it. Thirty-something was practically over the hill for a dancer. She needed to look at the big picture without blinders on.

"That's better." Sasha traded the curling iron for a blow dryer that she snapped on low. "Now raise your arms so we can dry your pits."

FILLED WITH SILK palm trees, real tropical flowers and colorful birds in cages, the chapel was decked out to resemble a garden paradise. A multitiered rock fountain splashed into a pool behind the minister. Nearly a dozen guests, including Nick's father, Salvatore, and sister, Caroline, were seated in rattan cushioned chairs. Vito Tolentino, who worked for Sally, was Nick's best man.

As happy as she was for Sasha and Nick, JoJo couldn't help feeling a little weird listening to the vows and seeing the rings being exchanged, as she'd planned on a wedding of her own a mere two months before. What a disaster marrying Mac Schneider—rather, Marco Scudella—would have been. He'd used her in his quest to get revenge on Nick, after murdering an uncooperative show girl Nick had once dated.

And JoJo was painfully aware that she might not have survived the honeymoon had there been one.

Ironically, only two men in her life had ever asked for her hand in marriage. A murderer and a man old enough to be her father. She remembered Oliver Phipps fondly, though. Actually, she'd thought of the lonely man as a substitute father—she'd lost her own as a kid. And he'd lost his daughter to cancer. They'd met when he'd helped finance a Broadway show she landed a part in, and they'd become immediate and fast friends.

"I now pronounce you man and wife," the minister intoned.

Before her, Nick pulled Sasha into his arms and kissed his new wife like a man crazy in love. JoJo swallowed hard and smiled, happy for the two of them. Oliver had asked her to marry him to keep her from leaving New York. She'd been flattered, but had gently turned him down because she hadn't loved him as a wife should love her husband. As Sasha so obviously loved Nick. And as she'd unfortunately loved the man who'd turned out to be Marco Scudella.

Cheers from the audience broke up the kiss. Both Sasha and Nick were grinning like fools.

"So let's party!" Sasha ordered.

The reception was held at the chapel, with a waiter and waitress passing out canapés and flutes of champagne.

"To the lovely bride and the lucky groom," Vito toasted.

Everyone lifted their glasses except Nick's sister, Caroline, who'd never liked any woman her brother showed too much interest in. Not even JoJo, though she and Nick had merely been good friends.

Caroline inched closer to JoJo, murmuring, "This is all your doing," in a scathing tone.

It gave JoJo the distinct feeling that Caroline *blamed* her for Nick's marrying Sasha. "I wish I could take the credit,'' she returned. "But Nick merely found Sasha irresistible.'' Caroline opened her mouth again, but JoJo forestalled her. "Maybe if you concentrated on your own life, you wouldn't have so much time to interfere with your brother's.''

Caroline gave her a look of pure poison and slipped away. JoJo was staring after her when a male voice too close to her ear startled her.

"I'd like to make a toast to you, too.''

JoJo whipped around and looked into eyes in a brilliant green shade that every member of the Donatelli family seemed to possess.

"What did I do?'' she asked Nick's father.

Sally gave her an intense look. "You went through lotsa grief a coupla months ago, and I feel responsible.''

"You weren't involved.''

"Not directly, no. But still... bad feelings between the Scudellas and Donatellis were born long before you.''

"My getting in the middle wasn't your fault,'' she assured him.

Sally Donatelli had been a big crime boss at that time, she knew, and though Nick had sought to legitimize the "family business'' while Sally was in jail, no one was certain exactly how well he'd succeeded. And Marco's father, Carmine, had been Sally's chief opponent in the old days. Maybe even now. She didn't want to know. She liked Sally, and since he was Nick's father, she wanted to keep on liking him.

"I have respect for you. You're a brave woman.''

"I don't feel very brave,'' she admitted. "I keep wanting to look over my shoulder wherever I go.''

"Maybe it's this town. Ever think about going back to New York City?"

"Not really. I miss people, not places. What's left of my family lives in Pennsylvania," she said, thinking of her mother and still-single younger brother. "And my best friends are right here." She saluted the newlyweds, who were locked in another clinch.

"You got good taste," Sally said expansively. "As does my son. They keep this up, and I'm gonna have grandkids sooner than I think."

JoJo laughed with him. They clinked glasses, finished their champagne and talked about the latest Elvis sighting, undoubtedly spread by a tourist who'd spotted one of the impersonators working Vegas.

A short while later, Sally moved on to talk to his son and the bride for a few minutes, while JoJo went in search of some appetizers. She'd calmed her empty stomach by the time the newlyweds caught up to her. JoJo noticed Nick's arm wound around Sasha's waist as if he were afraid she might disappear if he let go. As if Sasha would let him out of her sight!

"Nicky has a surprise for you, JoJo," Sasha told her. "Actually, this was all Sally's idea—but it's an offer you won't be able to resist."

Wondering what Nick's father had come up with, JoJo said, "Really? So spill."

"Some time off at the family ranch," Nick told her. "You can stay as long as you want."

Astonished, JoJo asked, "You own a ranch?"

"With facilities for a handful of guests. It's a small working ranch in Arizona, not too far from Sedona. The economy being what it is, the place was floundering, so we tried keeping it afloat by taking paid guests. So far, it's been a hit-and-miss proposition. You might even have the whole house to yourself. The wranglers, foreman and the housekeeper live in other quarters."

Thinking about a change of scene in a "New Age" area known for meditation and spiritual rejuvenation lifted a growing weight from JoJo's shoulders. Maybe this was just what she needed.

"I didn't know Sally was into cattle," she said.

"Actually, Caroline and Lucky and I inherited the Macbride Ranch from our mother's family. We used to spend a lot of time there as kids."

She had heard about Nick's mysterious younger brother, Lucky. He'd disappeared from the Las Vegas scene long before JoJo had entered it. No one seemed to know his whereabouts or what he'd been up to for the past half-dozen years—except maybe for Sally, who'd put investigators on his son's tracks. And Sally wasn't talking. While Nick hadn't complained, JoJo knew he was disappointed that Lucky hadn't been around to be his best man.

"So what do you say?" Sasha demanded.

JoJo hugged her best friend and with a big grin crowed, "Yee-hah!" Then she kissed Nick noisily on the cheek and whispered in his ear, "You better make Sasha happy or you'll answer to me!"

Nick grimaced. "Well, then, I guess I don't have a choice."

Only when JoJo let him go did she realize Nick's sister, Caroline, was nearby, her expression disapproving as usual.

SHE'D MEANT to get an early start, but exhaustion more mental than physical demanded JoJo sleep in. Not knowing whether she'd be gone for a few days or a few weeks, as Nick and Sasha had urged, she filled her biggest suitcase and a carryall to boot. Map and keys to the ranch house in hand, she set off midway through the afternoon.

On the way to the used Cherokee that was her pride—she'd never owned any manner of vehicle while living in Manhattan—JoJo checked her mailbox. Stuffed full. Helping with the wedding had kept her too busy the past few days to see to the practical details of her life. And they could wait a while longer, JoJo decided.

She loaded the mail into a zippered compartment on the outside of her larger suitcase, vaguely noting an envelope with a New York postmark.

Then she was off on her two-hundred-mile-plus trek southeast into Arizona, stopping a couple of times to get coffee and to stretch her legs. It was at one of those rest stops that JoJo had the sensation of being watched again. Ridiculous, of course. No one but Sasha and Nick knew where she was going. No one could have followed her from Las Vegas.

Right?

She rubbed at the back of her neck. A look around the parking lot at the half-dozen empty vehicles reassured her. Still, she drove off like a madwoman, checking her mirrors to see if anyone followed. When no car swung behind her, she relaxed.

Why couldn't she have left her imagination back in Nevada?

By the time she hit Flagstaff, JoJo was driving with country music blasting and her window down, delighted by the cooler mountain air. Rather than taking the faster highway south, she chose the scenic route through ponderosa pine ending in a stunning sixteenmile drive through Oak Creek Canyon. Lush pine forest melded into red-rock country, the trip down to the lower elevation executed on hairpin curves and a series of switchbacks. The sun was just setting, turning the surrounding rock to molten copper.

At the bottom of the canyon, JoJo pulled off the road to gawk while sections of the rock walls flared to life in shifts as the sun plunged below the horizon. The breeze played through the poplars and sycamores, their rustle hypnotic. Propped against the hood of her truck, inhaling earth-scented fresh air and enjoying nature's show while other vehicles sped by, JoJo felt some of the residual tension flow from her limbs.

It made her believe the area really did have the healing properties it was known for.

Her stomach rumbled. JoJo realized she needed something else, as well. Food. No reason she couldn't stop in Sedona for a real dinner, even if it would be getting dark soon. Nick had given her a detailed hand-drawn map, showing her how to get to the Macbride spread.

As she drove toward town, she thought about her phone call to the ranch the night before. The housekeeper, Flora Ramos, had confirmed that the extended family booked at the ranch would leave Sunday afternoon, and no one was scheduled in until the following Friday, so JoJo would have the house all to herself for nearly a week. Since she had warned Flora to expect her, surely the housekeeper would keep a light burning.

DRIVING DOWN the gravel path from the side road, JoJo tried not to get spooked again. The surrounding darkness was thick, its inky blackness relieved only by a sliver of moon and a dusting of stars overhead. No man-made lights had guided her since she'd left Sedona except those on her truck.

She switched on her high beams just in time to see the fork in the road. The map indicated she should veer left. Another quarter of a mile, and she spotted the sprawling, darkened, modern log ranch house.

Deciding she'd better figure out where things were before she unloaded, JoJo climbed out of the truck with no more than the house keys in hand. The main door was in the center of the long building, bedroom wings stretching out on each side. She unlocked the front door and opened it to more darkness. A switch to her left turned on a table lamp that softly lit the area, the large main room of the house.

JoJo looked around the pine-paneled room. On one wall, a big stone fireplace was flanked by two overstuffed plaid sofas and a set of matching chairs and ottomans. Heavy wooden coffee and end tables completed the living area, beyond which was a breakfront and a long wooden table and chairs for dining, plus an open kitchen area with iron skillets hanging over the old-fashioned stove.

She chose to explore the left wing for a bedroom. It had a short hallway with three doors, the one on her right open. She started to check it out. An indistinguishable noise made JoJo hesitate a moment in the doorway and listen hard. The sound was not repeated. Before she could get herself all worked up again—she was supposed to be relaxed here, for Pete's sake!—JoJo told herself the noise had to have come from outside, perhaps some nocturnal animal activity.

Continuing her exploration, she flipped the wall switch to reveal a large bedroom with a small sitting area and a private bathroom, all decorated in desert pastels. Pleased, she decided to claim the room and leave the rest of the house for the morning. But upon trading the room for the hall, she hesitated yet again, the strangest feeling chasing her, as if she weren't alone.

But she *was* alone, she reminded herself. No guests had been scheduled for the week. No car had been parked outside. No signs inside warned her of any other presence. Yet this inexplicable and thoroughly phantom feeling tracked her, not so different from what she'd been experiencing over the past few weeks. Ghosts that had followed her from Vegas in her mind.

Shaking away the spooky feeling, she proceeded to her truck to get her things.

A few minutes later, bags tucked in a corner of her room, JoJo thought to find something cool to drink to relieve her parched throat. But the moment she stuck a booted toe in the hall, her upper arm was caught in a firm vise that spun her around so fast it made her dizzy.

"Who the hell are you?" demanded a sleep-gruff voice.

Heart pounding in her throat, JoJo couldn't speak. Her back was pressed against a wall, and a half-naked man loomed over her. He was lean but muscular, the hair dusting his chest disappearing into the V of his unsnapped jeans. When she forced her gaze higher, to his face, it wasn't to a pretty picture. Broken nose, scarred chin and forehead, broad mouth pulled into a straight line, pale eyes flat.

Beneath sleep-mussed, burnished brown hair, he looked dangerous.

She lost her voice for a moment.

"I want to know who you are," he reminded her.

Gathering her courage, JoJo returned, "Who the hell are *you?*"

"Who wants to know?"

"No one was supposed to be here."

"Who said?" He was starting to sound exasperated.

"The housekeeper."

"You a friend of hers?"

"Are *you?*"

"If you won't tell me who you are, I'll just find out for myself."

Before her amazed eyes, he stormed into her bedroom and immediately spotted her purse at the foot of the bed. He went straight for it.

When he unzipped the bag, JoJo's temper flared. "Hey, what do you think you're doing?"

"Looking for your driver's license." He plunged his large hand into the bag and scooped out her wallet.

"Give me that."

He raised his arm, and though the wallet was out of her reach, JoJo went for it...and found herself brushing up against him. He was solid as a rock, and as warm as if he'd been baking under a noonday sun. JoJo's breath caught in her throat. The man's pale gray eyes lit with interest, and she flew back into the dresser.

"My name's JoJo Weston," she said, holding out her hand for her property. Her knees were shaky and her pulse was hammering in her throat. "Now, give me that."

But he'd already opened the wallet and had found her driver's license. "JoJo Weston. Five feet, seven inches. Hundred and twenty-four pounds," he read, then checked her out as if to make certain those were the facts.

JoJo squirmed. "Satisfied?"

He continued. "Brown eyes. Red hair. That natural red?" He didn't wait for an answer, but read her address. "Las Vegas, huh?" When they met hers again, his eyes burned with an odd light. "Who sent you?"

"Sent me?"

"Do you always answer questions with more questions?"

"Are you always so buffoonish?"

His deepened scowl made her think she'd pushed a bit too far. "Buffoonish? That's a word?"

"Now look who's talking in questions," she muttered.

He stepped closer and demanded, "What the hell are you doing here?"

The last was a shout that made JoJo shake inside. Why was he so angry? And what was she doing, standing for this interrogation? Why wasn't she running?

JoJo realized she was alone in a house with a man who could very well be violent. She hadn't the faintest idea of how far she'd have to run to reach the staff housing. The keys to the Cherokee were in her purse, and he was between it and her. And she hadn't even noted the location of the telephone, so she couldn't call for help.

Praying the man wasn't dangerous, she resorted to reason. "The owner of this place gave me free rein, okay? Who let you in?'' He could be an unexpected guest, after all.

A charged silence was followed by his, ''My keys let me in. *I'm* the owner.''

For a moment, JoJo feared she'd gotten herself turned around in the dark and had driven onto the wrong property. Good Lord, that would make her a burglar. Visions of her sitting in a jail cell danced in her head. But no, the keys Nick gave her fit the front door. So the man was lying. Undoubtedly *he'd* broken in, maybe through a window.

Looking around for some makeshift weapon, just in case, she asked, ''This is the Macbride Ranch, agreed?'' The only thing that came to mind was the lamp on the dresser, and it was plugged into the wall.

''What if it is?''

''I got the keys from Nick Donatelli himself.''

''Nick. Ah-h-h.''

Hearing the wealth of understanding in that sound, she stared at him and saw the knowing look in his expression. It didn't take a genius to know what he was thinking. The misconception irritated her, made her focus on righteous indignation rather than fear.

''Don't get any wrong ideas, here! I'm Nick's friend. And his new wife's best friend.''

He gaped. ''When did my brother get married?''

''Yesterday.'' Then it hit her and she went wide-eyed. ''Brother? You're not—''

''Lucian Donatelli.''

He didn't look a bit like Nick or Caroline or Sally. All three had green eyes and dark hair and smooth good looks that escaped this man. ''You wouldn't want to show me *your* driver's license?''

His grin was wolfish, intimidating. "You're free to look for one."

He raised his arms, inviting her to search his person. JoJo was tempted just to teach him a lesson. And if she didn't think he'd like her pawing him, she might have done it, too. The thought of touching him sent a rush of confusion through her, and heat seeped up her neck.

When she stayed put, he said, "Maybe you'd like to check out my bedroom?"

"Does a line like that work often?"

"Often enough. They call me Lucky—"

"Yeah, bad luck."

"Maybe you need to find out for yourself." He stepped closer.

Her hand shot out to stop him, the heel catching him in the solar plexus. Surprised when he flinched, she said, "Keep your distance."

He neither agreed nor tried to overpower her. But the look he gave her... When she refused to remove her hand, tension stretched between them.

JoJo didn't know what kind of a game Lucky was playing—if, indeed, he was Nick's brother as he claimed. He didn't look like Nick, certainly, but there was something about him. A male strength that was undeniable and powerful and very, very disturbing. Her palm on his flesh warmed, and her fingers tingled. Suddenly overheated, her body beading with perspiration, JoJo couldn't stand it any longer.

"Can we call it a draw?" she asked finally.

Tension visibly flowed from Lucky, and he backed off. "I assume you'll be leaving in the morning."

JoJo wanted nothing more than to be back in Las Vegas where she'd be safe.

Only she wasn't safe there, she reminded herself.

She only hoped she would be here.

"Your brother...Nick...invited me to stay here as long as I want," she said stubbornly.

"Suit yourself."

The way he said it made her think she might be sorry if she did. "I will," she said anyway.

With a black grin, he nodded, his tone ominous when he said, "See you in the morning, then."

JoJo refused to give him the satisfaction of seeing the doubt that flickered through her. She waited until he'd left her room and was on the way to his before rushing to close and lock the door.

His low laughter trailing down the hall got to her anyway.

An unladylike curse escaped JoJo, and she vowed to remain awake all night. Then, in the morning, she would find out whether or not her unexpected company really was Lucky Donatelli, as he claimed.

Chapter Two

"He introduced himself as Lucian Donatelli when he arrived late yesterday afternoon," Flora Ramos told JoJo the next morning when she entered the kitchen area where the housekeeper was making a huge breakfast of sausage, eggs and pancakes. "I had no reason to think he was lying."

JoJo poured herself a mug of coffee and wondered if the man in question was still sleeping. Glad that she had the opportunity to talk to Flora alone, she asked, "Then you never met him before?"

"I've only worked here for two years. I've met Mr. Nicholas and Miss Caroline, but never Mr. Lucian. *Dios,* if I've made a mistake and allowed a thief to move in..."

The housekeeper nervously smoothed her hair, blue black with a touch of silver at the temples. The sunny smile that had greeted JoJo first thing had evaporated. In her mid-forties, Flora Ramos seemed to be very sweet and very conscientious. Realizing the poor woman was working herself into a case, JoJo tried to reassure her.

"Don't upset yourself. He might very well be who he says he is. I just wanted to make sure since Nick told me I'd have the place to myself until Friday."

And there was no way to confirm Lucky's identity since Nick and Sasha were on their honeymoon, JoJo thought. No way would she ask anything of Sister Caroline of the Rotten Attitude. And while she liked Sally, JoJo didn't feel comfortable calling him, either. Too much had passed between the former crime boss and his younger son, or Lucky never would have disappeared in the first place.

"Surely someone here must have met Lucian Donatelli before."

Flora fetched a large oval plate and started loading it with the cooked food. JoJo had noticed the table was set for three people. Did the housekeeper plan on eating with her and Lucky—assuming the man presented himself any time soon?

"Only Vincent Zamora is around to take care of the extra horses," Flora told her. "The foreman, Henry Tidwell, has worked here for many years, but he took the wranglers out to the far range to bring in strays— the cattle graze on national forestland, you know. The men may be gone for the rest of the week." She thought for a moment. "Hmm, this stranger did stop by my place yesterday to let me know he'd arrived, and he did have his own keys. And the other man called him Lucky."

"What other man?"

"Eli something. He's staying in the wranglers' quarters—that's the old, original Macbride ranch house. It's on the other road cutting across the property, near my place." Flora brought the platter to the table, JoJo following. "Anyway, there was a vacant room, and Eli said he'd be more comfortable there than in some fancy house.''

JoJo came to terms with the fact that the man who'd nearly scared the wits out of her the night before might really be Nick's brother. Maybe. And even if he was, it wouldn't fully ease her mind. Why would Lucky show up here at the ranch after all these years? Why now? Was he up to something?

Still unsettled, she couldn't quite give up her inquisition. ''But you don't know who this Eli is supposed to be?''

''Eli Burke's a friend and business associate,'' came a curt reply. ''If you want to know more about him, ask me.''

Startled, JoJo whipped around to find Lucky coming straight for her from the front door. So he'd been up and around rather than sleeping.

She couldn't take her eyes from him.

He was attempting a casual posture that didn't hide the slight limp she hadn't noticed the night before. He was fully dressed—jeans, white T-shirt, leather vest and cowboy boots. Daylight was less kind to him than artificial light. She saw with perfect clarity the imperfections of his face. The broken nose. Forehead dominated by a still-pink scar, obviously new. The older white slash across his chin, contrasting with his deep tan, more prominent than she'd remembered.

And yet he wasn't an unattractive man. Besides which, he was well built and exuded an inexorable strength from within. The kind of man that made a woman stand a little taller, breathe a little deeper. The kind of man who intruded on a woman's early-morning dreams...and after she'd determined to stay awake all night, too.

JoJo forced away the fleeting memory and sank down into a chair at the table. "What kind of business?" she asked, referring to his relationship with the mysterious Eli.

"We've worked together."

Lucky drew out the chair across from hers and slid into it. The housekeeper set an insulated pot of coffee on the table between them, gave them both cautious looks and backed off.

"At what?" JoJo continued.

"Different things."

Entertaining fantasies of some young ruffian hooking up with Lucky for all manner of illicit schemes, she raised her eyebrows. "You could be more specific."

"And you could keep your nose to yourself."

"This from a man who ransacked my purse last night," she complained to Flora.

But upon looking around, she realized the housekeeper was slipping out the back door. Undoubtedly, their bickering had made the woman uncomfortable.

"So, you packed or what?"

"What?" she muttered, reaching for the food.

Lucky beat her to it, whipping the platter into his own possession. He began heaping large quantities of everything onto his plate.

If he thought his being rude would chase her off, he was mistaken, JoJo thought, giving him a filthy look. And if he ate all of the food, she would just march over to the stove and cook more herself. But he eventually gave over, and she saw there was enough left for two of her.

"You don't have any intentions of leaving, do you?" Lucky asked.

"I'm not going anywhere until I'm good and ready," she informed him.

A devilish grin twitched at his lips. "Maybe that'll be sooner than you think."

Was that a warning? Why did he want her to leave so badly, anyway? Alarm flared through JoJo even as she geared up to ask him. But the question never left her mouth. The front door opening interrupted her thoughts.

"Hey, mornin'!"

Lucky glanced over his shoulder. "Eli."

JoJo took stock of Eli Burke. Not exactly what she'd expected. In his late fifties, he was lean and tough, tanned and leathered. And more than a little bowlegged, to boot. The moment he spotted JoJo, he removed his perspiration-stained Stetson. She noticed that he was balding. And that his hazel eyes were friendly on her.

"Well, well... Lucky, you old son of a bull, you," Eli said, his voice sounding naturally hoarse. "Found yourself a pretty woman already, did you? What'd you do, slip out to town last night?"

JoJo gaped. He thought she... that Lucky and she... that they were *together?*

"We had an unforgettable encounter," Lucky agreed. "Didn't we, sweetest?"

She gave him a sickly sweet smile. "If you're trying to take away my appetite, don't bother." To prove that he couldn't shake her, she began stuffing her mouth.

"Ah, and she has a sharp tongue on her. Good girl! I'm Eli Burke, little darlin'," the older man said, claiming the empty spot at the head of the table. "Don't you mind Lucky none. He likes to tease, is all."

"Does he?" Threaten was more like it, if anyone wanted her opinion.

"That he does." Eli poured himself a cup of coffee, then reached for the remaining eggs, pancakes and sausage, sniffing loudly. "I'm starving. How's the chow?"

"Good enough for an old dog like you."

"See what I mean?"

"Yeah, he's a barrel of laughs."

Throughout breakfast, however, Eli was the one who made JoJo laugh over stories of his misadventures, first in the Texas oil fields, then on a New Mexican ranch and finally on a rodeo circuit that covered most of the states west of the Mississippi.

"I worked as a rodeo clown," he said, "which made me a target for angry broncs and bulls. Someone had to save his hide when he got himself into trouble," he said, pointing a thumb at Lucky.

He'd mentioned Lucky several times in those tall tales, so JoJo got the feeling they were partners of a sort, had been hanging together for years. No wonder Lucky seemed to have "disappeared," JoJo thought. He'd merely kept moving so often that it would be difficult to track him down. If he *was* Lucian Donatelli, she reminded herself. Eli could be part of some scheme....

"You shoulda seen Lucky with that bull," Eli was saying about some recent rodeo. "Any rider with a lick a sense woulda known when to let go and cover his, uh, britches. But not Lucky. That mean old Bushwhacker worked himself into a corner, then gave our friend here what for against the boards. That's how he got that pretty decoration on his forehead."

JoJo felt nearly relaxed for the first time since arriving at the Macbride Ranch. She had to admit she liked Eli. But a quick look at Lucky told her he was irritated with his buddy, as if he preferred to remain an enigma. The pink scar nearly glowed against his dark expression, and he looked as if he was working up to something unpleasant.

"Well, I'm full," JoJo said, pushing away from the table before Lucky could take out his bad spirits on her. Eli had put her in a good mood, and she meant to stay that way. "If you'll excuse me, I think I'll walk off some of this food, then maybe go for a ride."

"Don't get lost," Lucky said dryly.

Leaving JoJo with the distinct impression that that's exactly what he'd like her to do.

If Eli Burke had been an unexpected ray of sunshine in her morning, Vincent Zamora was a darker cloud than Lucky. When she went to see about getting herself a horse to ride, the cocky young wrangler looked her over through slitted black eyes that undressed her.

"Already heard about you," he said.

Which made her wonder who'd been talking. Lucky? Is that what he'd been up to before breakfast?

"Good things, I hope," she said casually.

"*Interesting* things."

Vincent's tone was as oily as the black hair straggling from the back of his hat along his neck. He smiled, his twisted mouth lascivious rather than inviting. JoJo had the distinct impression that he was barely holding back from smacking his lips over her.

From his swagger, she also gathered he thought he was something she wouldn't be able to resist.

"So you're a real, live Vegas show girl, huh?"

The way he said it made her skin crawl, as if he thought what she did for a living was sordid.

"I'm a dancer, yeah," she informed him. "I worked Broadway musicals for years. I moved to Nevada because I needed a change of scene."

"Oh, right."

Irritated, JoJo said, "My horse?"

He pointed to a thick-bodied gray mare sunning herself in the pasture behind him. "How about her?"

"She looks a little old and slow."

"Good beginner's horse."

"I'm not exactly a beginner."

While growing up, she'd visited her grandparents' farm during summer vacations and had ridden every horse on the property. Plus, she'd had enough opportunities to go riding over the years—including in Central Park—to know that she hadn't forgotten what she'd learned. Looking over the pasture, she found a horse whose looks she liked, a pretty little chestnut with some spirit. The mare was prancing and tossing her head as though she meant to show off.

"How about her?"

Vincent looked from the horse to JoJo. "Whatever you say." The mean twist to his mouth was back.

His remark gave JoJo some pause. "She *is* broken, right?"

"Right."

But the way he said it made JoJo a little nervous. Still, she wasn't about to back down.

Retrieving a saddle and leathers from a nearby shed, Vincent set them on a split rail of the fence and pro-

ceeded through the gate into the pasture. The land here
was flat, unlike the gentle rolls that gave way to hills
beyond. Nearly a dozen horses were pastured. Some
grazed, while others took shelter from the sun in the
shade of a live oak or under the long lean-to, where the
water trough and feed barrels had been set. JoJo
clambered onto the fence to watch while the wrangler
caught and tacked up the chestnut.

And every so often, she glanced back, expecting to
see Lucky Donatelli striding from the house, past the
barn and other outbuildings, to continue his one-man
crusade of giving her a hard time. Because of the nature of her ''glamorous'' job, she was used to dealing
with difficult men, though none had ever gotten to her
the way Lucky had. The thought that he might actually show up any minute made her pulse lurch—why,
being a mystery to her.

A few minutes later, Vincent passed her, mare in
tow. ''Okay, here she is.''

JoJo clambered down from the fencing and took the
reins the moment he led the mare through the gate
opening. ''What's her name?'' she asked as the horse
did a little dance before settling down.

''Spitfire.''

''Spitfire,'' she echoed, rubbing the mare's nose.
''Now, that's an interesting title.'' JoJo let the chestnut nuzzle her arm and chest to get acquainted while
she ran her free hand along the fiery mane. ''We redheads get an unfair reputation for temper, don't we?''
she murmured into the nearest ear, which twitched in
response.

Hoping the mare wasn't quite as spicy as her name,
JoJo took a big breath and mounted. Spitfire pranced
as would any spirited animal, but JoJo sat back and

held the horse together with firm legs and a steady hand. The mare quieted under her.

And Vincent's dark eyes registered his surprise.

But rather than congratulating her, he said, "You get turned around out there, you use those mule ears as a marker to get back."

He pointed to a high rock formation a short distance away that, if one got fanciful, could represent a mule's head with big, crooked ears.

Remembering Lucky's warning, she assured him, "I have no intentions of getting lost."

"A lot of country out there."

JoJo turned Spitfire and set off. She decided to be extra cautious and not wander far if for no other reason than not wanting to be on a horse too long her first time out. Too much time in the saddle, and she wouldn't be able to walk in the morning.

She skirted the ranch buildings and an enclosed stockade that lay between them and the house, passed a small apple orchard and a neglected vineyard. The scene that unfolded and spread out before her was dazzling. The land dipped into a low valley, edged by a high rock rim.

Taking a well-worn path in that direction, JoJo got in tune with her mount and with the beauty surrounding her. But something kept her from relaxing fully. Something that didn't feel quite right. The back of her neck prickled. She looked behind her, expecting to see Vincent staring after her. He'd disappeared. She slid her gaze in the direction of the house, wondering if the windows had eyes.

So what if they did? So what if Lucky were watching her?

JoJo chided herself. Her recent experiences had made her too suspicious of men's motives.

Better to concentrate on Mother Nature. Having loved the outdoors since those days on her grandparents' farm, she'd picked up some books on the flora and fauna of the Southwest months ago and was pleased to recognize the many life forms she'd read about but had had little occasion to see in person except for a few excursions from Las Vegas.

The valley was dotted with chaparral, low-growing plants like the red-barked manzanita and agave, shrub oak and hackberry. From the bottom of the valley, rolling hills ascended again, eventually giving way to rock formations. The rich green of white pine, gambel oak and dwarf maples contrasted sharply with buff-and-red sandstone.

Leaning forward in her saddle to ease Spitfire's burden as they took a steep incline, JoJo was startled by a loud crack from somewhere behind them. The mare flattened her ears, whinnied and lost her footing, and would have jounced JoJo loose from the saddle if she hadn't reacted quickly, tightening her quad muscles and hanging on for all she was worth.

"C'mon, Spitfire, settle down," she begged, stomach churning, not wanting the ignominious honor of having to walk back. "Thatta girl."

No sooner did the mare regain her footing and composure and make the lunge to more-even ground, than another sharp crack set the horse off again. This time, JoJo had a hell of a time trying to get her under control. Spitfire lowered her head and bucked and twirled. But JoJo could be as stubborn as any horse. Heart pounding, she clung desperately to the saddle and, realizing Spitfire had the bit between her teeth, didn't try to muscle her using the reins. Instead, she hung on and made soothing sounds until the mare collected herself and eased her jaw open, letting go of the bit to JoJo's relief.

"That's it, settle down."

JoJo's heart still raced, however, as she patted the sweat-slicked chestnut neck and looked around for the source of those noises that had spooked the horse. And her. Nothing. No one. Her stomach tied itself in knots as she wondered what the heck was going on. If she didn't know how unsettled she'd been lately, she'd think she'd heard gunshots.

If so, they hadn't been aimed at her, JoJo assured herself. The sounds had echoed from some distance. No earth or rock had churned anywhere near her as would have happened if struck by a bullet. Perhaps they hadn't been gunshots at all. Her imagination was turning into paranoia.

And that worried her.

This was supposed to be a rest cure, a way to center herself, and yet she hadn't had a moment's real ease since setting foot on the Macbride Ranch. What was happening to her? Was she losing it, headed for a nervous breakdown? Maybe it was the lack of sleep.

For JoJo could understand why she'd been so jumpy in Las Vegas...but no one around here had any reason to mean her harm.

THE SHOW GIRL WAS nearly as good a rider as she was a dancer. How surprising.

Not so surprising was the fact that JoJo Weston was acting as though she hadn't made any enemies. She merely gathered her horse under her and set off as if she didn't have a care in the world. Now that she wasn't in the spotlight, she could show her true colors, be her arrogant self.

For as long as she lived, that was.

The high-powered binoculars lowered as she disappeared around a curve. No matter. Plenty of time to be up close and personal. Plenty of time to contemplate the many ways a tenderfoot could die. A gloved hand lifted the still-warm rifle that had been aimed at the heavens when fired. A bullet could have taken her down, of course, but that would have been too obvious when more subtlety was called for.

A tragic accident.

How thoughtful of her to leave Las Vegas, to choose a place that was perfect in its very isolation. If something unexpected were to happen to the bitch out here, who would ever suspect that her demise had been carefully planned?

More important, who would ever care?

HOURS LATER, after a late-morning nap in a shady place along a creek that crossed the property, a rested and calmed JoJo rode right up to the pasture where Vincent seemed to be waiting for her. He let her dismount before taking Spitfire's reins.

"Have yourself a good one?"

"Beautiful country."

"Your lasting so long on Spitfire is a real feat. Don't get fooled, though. Danger lurks in unexpected places out there."

Starting, JoJo wondered if she should be reading a deeper meaning into Vincent's statement. Surely not.

"I'm always careful," she assured the wrangler.

If there were another meaning to his words, he didn't let on. He merely gave her an oily smile before leading Spitfire over to the fence.

JoJo watched him loosen the cinch, then turned and jogged back to the ranch house to find the grounds eerily quiet. Next to her cherry red Cherokee sat a dark and dour sedan that she figured belonged to Lucky. It didn't seem like the type of vehicle he'd drive, but then she'd been fooled by assumptions based on outer trappings before.

Upon entering the house, she had cause to stop in mute surprise. A man with thick dark blond hair and perfect good looks was staring back at her from the breakfront where he poured himself a drink.

He lifted his glass in salute. "Hey, there, you must be JoJo."

"Do I know you?" Something about him seemed vaguely familiar.

"Flora told me your name. Said you and that Lucky fellow were the only people here right now other than me. Can I get you a drink?"

"No, thanks. Alcohol would only put me to sleep, Mr...."

"Name's Adair Keating."

"You're alone?" she asked, thinking it odd he'd appeared out of nowhere.

He grinned, his teeth white against his tan. "All by my lonesome. I work as a stuntman. Just finished shooting some hard riding scenes for a new Western, *Call of the West,* this morning. Maybe you saw us over by Cathedral Rock."

"Actually, I've been riding myself around here today."

"Nice place. I wasn't in a rush to get back to the earthquakes and floods and brushfires in Los Angeles, and one of the locals told me about the Macbride Ranch. I figured I'd check it out."

"Then you're just here for the day?"

"At least a few days. I haven't decided how long, actually." He sauntered toward her. "Thought I'd play it by ear. I'm an impulsive kinda guy."

Staring into his blue eyes gave her a funny feeling. "I swear I've seen you before."

"Maybe in a movie."

He did have movie-star looks, even though he was only a stuntman. "Maybe...but I was thinking more like in person. When was the last time you were in Las Vegas?"

He hesitated only a moment before saying, "Right before this assignment. We mighta passed each other in a casino or something."

"Or something." Unable to place him, JoJo started for her room. "I need to get cleaned up before I go into town. I smell like horse."

"Flora said she'll have dinner ready at seven. You will be back? I hate eating alone."

Though she'd figured on getting a bite in town after hitting some of the galleries, Adair's hopeful expression was so charming she changed her mind.

"I'll be here," she promised. "Though be prepared for a rain cloud."

"You really think it's going to rain?"

"A figure of speech," JoJo clarified—she was thinking of Lucky's making an appearance.

And she couldn't help but wonder where the mystery man had gotten himself off to in the meantime.

LUCKY PORED OVER the intricate plans spread across the table in the Wrangler's Roost, as the old ranch house had been nicknamed. The place was well-worn but comfortable and, thanks to several additions, provided a private room for each of the men who lived on the property. And since those men were gone for a few days—all except Zamora, who was busy seeing to the horses and repairs on the outbuildings—the Roost gave them the privacy they needed.

"So what do you think?" Eli asked, leaning back in the heavy wood chair across from Lucky.

They'd been working on the plans all morning, but no matter how he looked at it, Lucky came to the same conclusion. "It's gonna take more up-front money than we have."

"You got resources."

"No."

"Hey, the old man would be proud."

"I don't want him to be proud. I don't want anything to do with him."

"Aah!" Sounding disgusted, Eli swiped the air with an open hand. "You got some serious thinking to do."

"I've had years to think on it," Lucky said calmly.

"But this is your shot, man. *Our* shot. Makes all the other jobs we've done kids' stuff."

"But we've done them on our own."

"And what have we got to show for it?"

"Independence. A family's supposed to be made up of parents and their kids, not a whole organization. If I can't have one without the other..."

Not that Eli hadn't heard Lucky's opinion before. They never had agreed on this one. Eli was an old-time grifter at heart. He'd never pass up a likely opportunity. Then again, he'd always been small-time, had never dealt with the likes of Sally Donatelli.

"You got to think about the future," Eli was arguing. "And what you're owed."

He was starting to sound like a broken record. Lucky felt his temper rising, but kept it in check. He needed Eli. He couldn't do this alone. Rather, he didn't want to.

"Nothing is going to change my mind."

"Not even the woman?"

The woman.

Lucky couldn't believe his father's nerve. He'd known Sally had someone on his tail—he would have been surprised if it had been otherwise. But Sally didn't know his younger son if he thought a pretty face would bring him back to the fold. He wasn't Nick. No female was going to manipulate him on someone else's orders.

"Especially not the woman," he said finally. "So help me, before I'm through with her, JoJo Weston will wish she'd never left Las Vegas."

JOJO WAS STILL WONDERING about Lucky's whereabouts after a cozy dinner for two with Adair. She'd made Flora go home once the food was ready, insisting they could serve themselves and take care of the cleanup.

Adair Keating proved to be charming company, unlike that provided by the dour owner of the ranch. He seemed taken that they had show biz in common. JoJo felt as if she was doing all the talking, though, telling him about her favorite Broadway musicals. Somehow he never got around to telling her about his adventures in the movie trade.

And every so often, despite the gorgeous man's constant attention, JoJo found her mind wandering, speculating about what Lucky was up to.

She really did need to get her head examined.

"We could make a fire, have an after-dinner drink," Adair suggested as he scraped plates and she loaded them into the dishwasher.

"Thanks, but I'll pass. I'm bushed." She was tired, but more important, she felt the need for some time alone. "I haven't had a really good sleep in weeks, but I think tonight's the night."

"It's not even nine."

"And I'm not even unpacked." She added the dish detergent and started the washer. "I hate living out of a suitcase."

"Then I guess I'll see you at breakfast. Any idea of what you want to do tomorrow?"

JoJo figured she must be crazy, but she said, "I came alone to chill out. Know what I mean?"

"Uh-oh. You just broke up with a man."

"You nailed it." Not that she was about to give him details.

He made an apologetic gesture. "I didn't mean to intrude on your privacy."

"No, don't feel like that. I enjoyed dinner. Now I need some space."

"I got the picture."

And he didn't seem too disappointed, thank heavens. "Good night."

JoJo was as good as her word. She spent the hour unpacking and organizing her clothes and cosmetics. She was something of a neatnik. Too organized for Sasha all those years they'd shared a New York apartment. Grinning, she wondered how the honeymoon was going.

About to stuff the big suitcase in the closet, she remembered the mail she'd pulled out of her box on the way to the car. She unzipped the side compartment and emptied the contents onto the mattress. Once her bags were out of sight, she plopped down into the middle of the bed and began sorting mail. Bills. Magazines. Letters.

She read the missive from her mother first, friends next. Finally she got to an official-looking envelope from Abrams and Horowitz, a New York law firm. She set it on the spread and stared at it. Somehow, she didn't think she was going to like the contents—not that she would know until she read whatever was inside.

Grabbing it, JoJo ripped open the envelope, pulled out the letter and reluctantly began to read.

Dear Miss Weston:
With regret we must inform you of the passing of Oliver Phipps. On the morning of June 3, he had a massive heart attack and never recovered.
    Mr. Phipps regarded you highly and . . .

JoJo couldn't read the rest. Tears blurred her vision. She folded the letter and shoved it back in its envelope, as if by doing so, she could deny the contents. But she'd read enough. Dear Oliver dead. She could hardly believe it. He'd been old enough to be her father, certainly, but he'd had the spirit of a young man.

A spirit that was now gone forever.

And she'd never had the chance to say goodbye, hadn't contacted him once since she'd met the man she thought she was going to marry.

JoJo wept. Tears poured out of her until she was drained. Dehydrated.

She cleared the bed of the mail, got into a pair of loose, satiny pajamas and climbed under the covers. Memories assaulted her. An hour later, she was still staring up at the ceiling in the dark with no hope of sleep. That drink Adair had offered her sounded good right about now.

Rising, she rinsed her face with cold water and pushed at her messy red curls, too dispirited to do more.

The house was dark but for the soft glow of burning logs in the fireplace. Her gaze immediately went to the breakfront, her legs following automatically. Feeling numb inside, she opened the doors that hid the bottles of liquor.

"You could see better if you turned on the dining room light."

Her heart lurched as she whipped around to find Lucky sitting in a chair, staring at her.

"What are you doing, sitting in the dark like that?"

"Waiting for you," he said ominously.

Chapter Three

JoJo's hand shook as she poured herself a brandy, but she wasn't certain if her sudden nerves came from the bad news about Oliver or from the bad news sitting in the chair before the fire. If Lucky expected her to turn tail and run back to her room, he would be sadly disappointed. Instead, she took the chair opposite, curled one leg under her and let the bare toes of the other reach for the warmth of the fire.

A small sip of the brandy started a fire inside her, as well. She let the liquor trickle down her throat. The slow, syrupy warmth made her feel a bit better.

Gradually, her vision adjusted so she could see more than just a male silhouette created by the fire's glow. The golden light camouflaged Lucky's scars and softened his features. But the pale eyes that reflected flames at her were hard as agates. She noted he was drinking, as well.

Wondering if he were drunk, she finally asked, "So what made you think you'd see me tonight?"

Lucky sounded perfectly sober when he said, "I figured you'd scurry out of hiding as soon as you heard me come in."

"Are you really that arrogant or are you just pretending?"

"Why play games?"

"*I'm* not playing at anything. And I didn't have a clue you were anywhere around."

His laugh was low and harsh, raising the hair at the back of her neck. He was staring at her relentlessly, as if he had some reason to dislike her. Undoubtedly, it was her *type* he didn't care for. He probably preferred his women docile and deferential. He'd probably expected her to leave the moment he'd suggested she do so.

"If you're not playing games, then why," he asked, "did you come out, dressed so... provocatively?"

"What?" She glanced down at herself, half-expecting to see several buttons of her pajama top undone. But the garment was intact. "I wouldn't call my wearing a pair of loose pajamas provocative."

His stony gaze traveled down her length. Slowly. Lingered on her bare foot.

"You're a woman who knows what men like."

From what she could see of his expression, JoJo gathered Lucky was serious. She'd never thought of herself as some kind of femme fatale, but maybe the fact that she was a show girl sparked his fantasies... not that she'd told him what she did in Las Vegas. Somehow, he must have figured it out, though. Men didn't fall over themselves when they saw her, not as they did over the statuesque Sasha. Self-consciously, she pulled her free leg up, hugging it to her chest, placing something of a barrier between them.

"As I said, I had no clue that I wouldn't be alone." She took another sip of the brandy.

"So you drink alone often?"

"I rarely drink at all."

"Then why tonight?"

Not knowing why she chose to tell him, she said, "I just learned a friend of mine died." She sloshed the brandy around in its glass. "I was having trouble sleeping."

Silence. No wisecracks? JoJo was relieved. She looked up, realized Lucky was studying her, as if he were searching for the truth.

Finally, he nodded and said, "I'm sorry."

She sighed. "So am I."

"Want to talk about it?"

"No." Not to him with his smart mouth. But who else was there? And keeping it inside was already eating at her. "Yes," she said tentatively, thinking she would blow Lucky out of the water if he so much as said the wrong word. "His name was Oliver Phipps. Though his business was real estate rather than theater, he helped raise money for new productions. He loved Broadway musicals."

"And you loved him?"

"Very much. He was a good, kind person. A warm, caring man. He'd suffered a lot of tragedy—the deaths of his wife and only daughter—and yet he focused on the positives in life. He was an inspiration. It's impossible to be indifferent to someone like that."

"Then why did you leave him?"

JoJo recognized the tension in Lucky's question, as if he had a personal stake in the answer. Had some woman broken his heart when she left him? That could be why he'd been giving her such a hard time— on general principle rather than because of some more personal reason.

"I wasn't *in love* with him. Marrying a friend . . . it just wouldn't have been right."

"A lot of couples have less going for them."

"Maybe my expectations are higher," she said, and then thought about the way she'd let another man suck her in. "More likely, I'm just plain stupid."

Lucky had no comeback.

JoJo drained half her glass and stared into the fire as if flames could give her answers to questions she'd been asking herself for the past two months.

Maybe Lucky was right, and she'd made a big mistake turning Oliver down. But she'd wanted more than the quiet caring they'd had for each other. She'd wanted high romance, to be swept off her feet.

And that's exactly what Marco Scudella had done. In the guise of Mac Schneider, he'd fulfilled all her romantic fantasies. Their courtship had been whirlwind, and she'd been swept along without a single suspicion that he'd been using her to get at Lucky's brother.

So what did that say about her judgment?

Oddly enough, JoJo realized that while she felt betrayed, she wasn't brokenhearted, almost as if she'd known underneath that her relationship with the cheerful blackjack dealer had been too good to be true. Or maybe the very quickness of it all had cast a glow of unreality over the situation. The danger she'd put herself in had been very real. If it hadn't been for Lester imprisoning her to protect her, she would have married a murderer.

Wondering if any other woman had ever been so foolish, JoJo splashed back the rest of the brandy.

LUCKY FELT his animosity for JoJo Weston deflate a bit. It was hard to be angry with a woman who was so obviously mourning a man she'd cared about. A man with some means. A man she hadn't married, though she'd indicated he'd wanted to marry her. If she wasn't guided by money, what then? Everyone had motivation for their actions.

Lucky was too disenchanted with the whole business of romance to believe in the kind of love portrayed in books or movies. He'd been soured on the idea early in life. The women who'd gravitated to the Donatelli brothers had always wanted something from them. Usually things money could buy. Less often, influence. But always something.

His years away from Las Vegas hadn't taught him any different. His fancy had been caught by a few women, mostly on the rodeo circuit, but none who'd cared for him. They had stuck around not for what he could buy them—like the others—but because of the fake glamour attached to what he did for a living, his skill often making him the center of attention. A subtle kind of usery, but usery no less.

And JoJo Weston wouldn't be any different, he told himself. Her arriving at the Macbride Ranch directly after he had was no accident.

"So, are you going to the funeral?"

She gave him an odd look. "You'd do anything to get me off this property, wouldn't you?"

"If you really *cared* about your friend, I'd think you'd want to—"

"He died more than a week ago, so there's no funeral for me to go to." Sudden tears lent a sheen to her eyes.

Fearing she was about to cry, Lucky clamped his mouth shut. Nothing was more irritating than a bawling woman. JoJo sniffed a few times, took a deep breath and closed her eyes. When she opened them, they were still sad, but free of tears.

"I can't figure you for Nick's brother."

"What's to figure?"

"For one, he's a nice person."

"And I'm not?"

"If the shoe fits..."

He had to unclench his jaw to ask "What else?"

"Nick doesn't judge people so quickly."

"Who said I'm judging you?"

Her laugh was tinged with irony. "That's exactly what you've been doing from the moment you attacked me. Another thing—Nick's a gentleman."

"I didn't attack you."

"Do you always put your hands on strange women?"

He gave her a slow grin. "Some of them even like it."

"And you can't even be serious when it counts!"

"Why should it count, JoJo?" he pressed. "Why are you really here?"

"I told you—"

"Exactly nothing."

JoJo sighed. "Sorry if my presence bothers you. You're not driving me away from this ranch, but I guess we don't have to be in the same room."

She rose unsteadily, the brandy undoubtedly making her weave as if she might fall.

Instinctively, Lucky whipped out of the chair and grasped her arm. She started, and the empty glass fell to the Navajo area rug with a thunk. No doubt, she'd choose to put the worst light on this action, too.

"I wasn't trying to make you angry."

"Then you weren't doing a very good job," she said, a little catch in her breath.

The warmth of her flesh seduced his fingers. Lucky told himself to let go of her. His hand wouldn't obey. What the hell was wrong with him?

And why wasn't JoJo telling him to go to hell?

But JoJo wasn't saying anything. She was staring at him, lips parted, confusion and surprise warring with her sadness. A flush of firelight laved her features, making her seem almost beautiful.

His gaze dropped to the pulse beating visibly in her throat. And beneath the sleek peach material of her pajama top, her breasts rose and fell so seductively they forced a tightening in his groin. He couldn't rip his gaze from the sight, and as he stared, he could see her nipples harden through the thin material.

Her breath became audible. Uneven.

He was sexually attracted to her, and damn if she wasn't attracted right back!

Suddenly wary, Lucky forced his hand to open and drop to his side. JoJo remained still, as if waiting for his next move. She was tempting; he'd have to give her that. Despite the fact that he knew a nearby room was occupied, that Adair Keating might even be awake to hear, Lucky would like nothing more than to gather JoJo in his arms, tumble her to the floor and take her right there in front of the fire. His body was urging him to do so.

But maybe that was part of her plan. Seducing him. Maybe this story about the friend who'd died was made up to trick him, to lull him into trusting her. But if he knew that, if he were forewarned . . .

Before he could make up his mind about what to do, the scrape of a key against the front-door lock whipped him around. "Who the hell is that?"

The slight woman who pushed through the doorway with a suitcase half her size stopped with a squeak when she saw him. "Oh, Lord, you startled me!"

Lucky glared. "And you are?"

Her eyes widened. "Paula Gibson. Uh, did I come into the wrong house or something?"

"No," JoJo assured her. "Lucky just likes making women feel that way. He doesn't appreciate surprises."

Lucky thought her voice surprisingly flat considering the sexual tension that had just passed between them. "We weren't expecting you."

Paula hooked her straight, light brown hair behind an ear. "I called late this afternoon from Phoenix to see if there was an opening. Flora Ramos didn't tell you?"

"I wasn't around," Lucky said. "Sorry if I was rude."

"No problem." Paula shrugged. "It *is* late. I got lost, as usual. A complete lack of direction is my biggest shortcoming, I'm afraid. I had a map and wrote down how to get here and everything, but I could get lost in a paper sack, I swear." She rolled her eyes for emphasis and barely took a breath before going on. "Anyhow, I woke up the poor housekeeper to get the key. She asked me if I minded coming over here by myself since she wasn't dressed and all. She said I should just make myself at home. Pick an empty room."

When she started dragging her bag to the left, Lucky said, "Try the other wing. All kinds of rooms free there."

Though there was a vacant room in the wing he shared with JoJo, he didn't want to give up more of his privacy. A privacy that was starting to include her, he was afraid. Despite his good sense, he wanted her alone . . . or the next best thing to it.

"Sure. No problem." As she took a good look at JoJo's pajamas, Paula's eyebrows shot up. She scurried away, saying, "I promise I won't interrupt again. Go ahead and get back to whatever you were doing."

Nice thought, but the mood was broken. JoJo was picking up the brandy glass from the carpet, the movement exposing the pale swells of her breasts. Well, maybe not altogether broken, Lucky amended, catching his breath.

This was beginning to look like a cold-shower night.

"I JUST WENT THROUGH a lousy divorce," the chatty Paula was saying as they finished breakfast the next morning. "So I was moping around the office for a couple of weeks, and one of the other secretaries insisted I needed a getaway, so she told me about the Macbride Ranch. She spent a week here with her boyfriend last fall and couldn't stop raving about how beautiful the place was. I figured some R&R would do me good, and so here I am."

Here they all were, JoJo thought wryly. Lucky, Eli, Adair, Paula and yet another unexpected guest.

Rocky Franzone had shown up just after daybreak. He looked like a Rocky—broad and muscular, dark and swarthy. And from his accent, JoJo guessed he was originally from Jersey—though he was all duded up in Western clothes.

"I made plans to hook up with a buddy in the area on Saturday," he announced. "We're gonna get some work wrangling, so I figured a ranch is the perfect place to wait."

Nick's estimation of the ranch's low popularity quotient would have to be revised, JoJo thought.

Part of her had really wanted some time to chill out alone, but another part was glad of all the company that diffused the situation between her and Lucky. Who knew what might have happened between them the night before if Paula hadn't interrupted? Every so often, she caught him staring at her and figured he was wondering, too.

"So, what are we all going to do today?" Paula asked.

She drew her hair behind her ear with long pink-tinted nails and gave Lucky an expectant look. Over breakfast, Flora had informed everyone that he was one of the owners.

"No activities director," Lucky said. "This is a working ranch, not a dude ranch. Flora cooks breakfast and dinner, but other than that, you're on your own."

"You don't have any activities?" Paula asked.

"If you want a horse, a wrangler named Vincent Zamora will saddle one for you. He's already working down around the outbuildings."

Paula turned to JoJo. "Are you up for a ride?"

Despite her resolve to take it easy the first time out, she was a little stiff. "Maybe later."

"I hear you're a regular cowgirl," Lucky said. "What happened? Lose your enthusiasm for horses for some reason?"

Had Lucky been talking to Vincent or watching her? JoJo wondered. Irritated that he was trying to start something, she said, "Maybe I just know my limits."

"Smart lady—"

She cut him off. "You could use some limits yourself."

Dead silence followed, until Rocky turned to Paula. "You want company," he told the new divorcée, "I wouldn't mind getting on a nag and playing cowboy."

"Great." Paula smiled so wide her dimples popped. "So let's get going."

"Yip-ee-ai-ay!" Rocky crowed.

As Flora started to clear the table, Paula and Rocky left immediately, Lucky and Eli following, their heads together and talking in low tones as if they were plotting something. JoJo couldn't stop herself from staring after them. And just before he closed the door behind him, Lucky glanced back at her as if he felt her interest.

For a brief moment, their gazes locked, and JoJo felt the same way she had the night before—paralyzed by something she couldn't explain.

Then Lucky broke the connection and pulled the door shut. And JoJo started, wondering what in the world had gotten into her. The man was hardly trying to sweep her off her feet, and yet her pulse soared and chest tightened. She was vulnerable—that was all, she assured herself. And the indefinable something between them was her fear.

But fear of what? Of him? Or herself?

When it came to men, she'd proved her judgment wasn't the best....

"So what're your plans?" Adair asked from where he'd sprawled across a couch. "Just a friendly question. Don't worry—I'm not gonna horn in on your privacy again."

"Hey, it's okay," JoJo said quickly, a little embarrassed.

After telling the man she wanted her space the night before, she'd gotten all too close to Lucky. She only hoped Adair had been sound asleep, unaware of what had been going on mere yards from his bedroom.

"I was thinking I could stand to walk off some of that breakfast," she said. "When I was riding yesterday, I passed an apple orchard not too far from the house. It'll give me a good stretch."

"I thought I'd stretch out, too. Right here on this nice comfortable couch." Patting a stuffed pillow and putting it behind his head, he added, "I could use a few good winks. I'm a pretty light sleeper. Things just kept waking me up last night . . . including Paula's arrival."

"Things" being the obvious to JoJo. Warmth crept up her neck as she made for the door. "Well, I hope tonight's better for you. Later."

Mortification flooded her as she stalked rather than walked to the apple orchard, passing the outbuildings and the big enclosure without really seeing them. But by the time she arrived at her destination, she'd relaxed some. And she'd worked out the kinks in her legs and back.

JoJo sat for a while at the edge of the copse, just enjoying the clear air and sun and breeze. This tranquility was exactly what Dr. Sasha had ordered.

Used to the bustle of a big city, JoJo appreciated the quiet solitude of the outdoors. She always had. As a kid, she'd looked forward to those summers on her grandparents' farm. Growing up, busy building her Broadway career, she'd somehow forgotten how pleasurable it was just to do nothing. To be one with nature.

Not believing in regrets, JoJo didn't look back. Rather, she was looking forward. Time was beginning to press in on her, the urgency no doubt precipitated by the awful mess she'd gotten into with Marco and Lester.

She'd been brought face-to-face with her own mortality. If Sasha hadn't come to her rescue . . .

How ironic that she was in her early thirties and already worrying about retirement. She had at least a few good dancing years left in her, maybe more. But what about after that? A question not many young women with ambition asked themselves when starting out, JoJo thought. If only she'd saved more than a few bucks, she might be able to start some kind of small business. As it was, her options were limited.

At least she didn't feel so anxious when she strolled back the way she'd come. She identified plants and searched for the wildlife that scurried through the chaparral and managed to remain just out of sight. Attuned to the world around her, she was breathing deeply, humming to herself, when she heard the faint strains of music coming from somewhere ahead, in the general direction of the outbuildings. Undoubtedly Vincent was listening to the radio as he worked.

But as she drew closer, JoJo realized the melody was strangely familiar, because it was a tune used in the show at the Caribbean. As a matter of fact, the piece was a Latin rumba she knew well since it was *her* music... or rather, music she danced to with a partner.

How weird.

Compelled to investigate such an odd coincidence, JoJo followed the sultry strains directly toward the mysterious enclosure with its solid six-foot-high walls. Since she couldn't see in, she had no idea of what the thing was used for. Feed storage, maybe? The gate stood open, giving her the opportunity to check it out for herself.

She stepped inside.

"Hello? Vincent?" JoJo's eyes were drawn directly to the center of the large sandy floor and the boombox pumping out the rumba. "Hey, anyone around?"

Though no one answered, she wandered forward, her feet taking her toward the sound equipment. Had Vincent tuned into some Spanish-language station that played Latin music, or was he really listening to the score from the Caribbean's show? She supposed Nick could have left a tape around last time he was at the ranch.

JoJo crouched in front of the silver boombox, thinking to find out for herself if she was listening to a broadcast or a tape. She'd barely wrapped her fingers around the handle before a harsh blowing sound behind and to her left froze her in place. The hair at the back of her neck tingled when she heard the animal snort again, the sound followed by a deliberate pawing at the earth.

Swallowing hard, JoJo glanced over her shoulder and eyeballed what she'd missed upon entering the enclosure—a buff-colored hide blending nicely with the sandy earth.

An angry-looking Brahma bull fixed his beady eyes on her.

Chapter Four

"Uh-oh," JoJo muttered, her stomach clutching.

Rising, the boombox coming with her since the handle was still grasped tightly in her hand, she tried to gauge the distance between her, the snorting bull and the exit. But when she glanced back at the gate, she got a start. Undoubtedly not realizing anyone was inside, someone had shut the damn thing, and, no doubt, locked it to boot.

Great!

If the gate were locked, how the heck was she supposed to get out?

The bull really looked irritated. Outweighing her by several hundred pounds, the animal had a powerful humped neck wider than her hips, and curved horns that looked sharp enough to slice right through steel like butter. And if she weren't mistaken, bulls had pretty short tempers.

Sweat prickling at her skin, JoJo began backing up slowly, silently, so as not to aggravate him further.

The Brahma lowered his head anyway, snorting and pawing. Dust churned around him. His protracted moan bounced off the walls of the enclosure and straight down her spine.

She'd have to somehow vault over the six-foot fencing...if she could manage to hike herself up, that was. Thankfully, as a dancer, she was in great physical condition.

Suddenly, his wounded sound drowning out the music, the bull lowered his head and charged her.

And JoJo's body went on automatic. She turned and ran for all she was worth. Her boot scuffed something ragged in the sandy earth, nearly bringing her to her knees. Frantic, she made for the water trough in the corner of the pen, about three feet high, a stepping-stone to safety. She had to get to it before the bull got to her.

But the bull was closing the distance behind them faster than she was running. JoJo could hear his sides heave as he drove after her. Her fingers biting into the metal of the boombox, it suddenly hit her that she should get rid of the damn thing....

Instinct whipped her arm out, the weight of the equipment tearing at her shoulder, setting its own trajectory. She opened her fingers, and the boombox went flying. She heard a thud and an inhuman scream of outrage. Not pausing to see what happened, JoJo leaped up onto the water trough, wrapped her hands around the edge of the fence and vaulted up.

Scrambling one leg over, JoJo straddled the wood, throwing a glance back at the bull. He was no longer chasing her, for he had a more immediate concern. Head low, he attacked the boombox. One of his horns pierced the metal. He whipped around in a tight circle, shaking his head and bucking, trying to rid himself of the thing. To add insult to injury, the music was still playing.

The bull looked ridiculous, and even though her heart was beating too fast, JoJo couldn't help but be amused . . . and concerned that the beast would hurt himself.

As she watched, however, the Brahma stopped, legs spread, sides heaving, nose nearly touching the ground. Then he threw up his head with the full force of his powerful neck. The boombox flew into the air, flipped around in a spiral and dropped a slim yard to the side. Without losing a beat, he charged the offensive object, running right over it, his weight crushing the sound from the metal.

The arena went still but for the animal's snorts of triumph as, head held high, he circled his vanquished enemy.

Relieved that neither of them was hurt, JoJo dropped to the ground outside the enclosure. Her entire body suddenly felt like Silly Putty. Holding on to the wall for support, she let out the nervous laughter that threatened to choke her, more of a strangled sound than anything. Then she took several deep, slow breaths, and willed her pulse to steady.

But her heart received another unexpected jolt when an angry voice behind her demanded to know, "What the hell were you doing in there?"

Whirling around to face Lucky Donatelli, she said the first thing that came to mind. "Dancing." What did he think? "Didn't you hear the music?"

Furious that she'd barely missed being injured through no fault of her own, and that he was obviously blaming her, JoJo tried flouncing by Lucky, but her knees were weak, and one of them buckled slightly. Before she could right herself and regain her dignity, she felt a band of steel slide along her back and another behind her knees.

"Hey, what do you think you're doing?"

Without so much as a by-your-leave, Lucky was lifting her into his arms. "Manhandling you again," he growled.

Then he stalked across the yard, muttering what she figured were obscenities under his breath. But no matter that he was in a vile mood—a seemingly natural state for him—and no matter that his rough, no-nonsense demeanor scared her more than a little, JoJo recognized the same thread of attraction to him that had caught her the night before.

Something about being trapped against his big hard belt buckle was inviting, sent unbidden warmth spiraling through her. Or maybe it had to do with the way he looked in faded, butt-hugging jeans and a white cotton T-shirt with the sleeves ripped out. The desire to run her fingers along a well-muscled arm was more tempting than she wanted to admit.

Instead—convinced the run-in with the bull was impairing her judgment, making her act like a weak-spirited ninny—JoJo pushed at Lucky's chest and tried to untangle her legs from the death grip he had on them. No matter how hard she tried to make him let her down, however, he didn't budge. He didn't even lose a beat.

"I can walk. You can put me down." When he ignored her, she worked up some righteous indignation. "What's the point of hauling me around like a sack of feed?"

"Saving the ranch from a lawsuit in case you twist your ankle or something on the way back to the house."

Or something. She envisioned the bull charging her.
"You should have thought about that before."

"Before what?"

"Before . . . before someone left the gate to that enclosure open!" she sputtered.

"And you were reckless enough to wander inside?
Are you out of your mind, tangling with a bull?
Bushwhacker's not a pet. And he's damn danger-
ous!"

"Tell me about it."

He *was* blaming her. Wait a darn minute. *Bushwhacker?* The name was familiar, one that had been
imparted by Eli. Her gaze traveled to the pink scar on
Lucky's forehead barely peeking from beneath his
cowboy hat.

"Isn't this the bull who fancied you up?" she asked,
pointing to the scar.

"One and the same."

"And you own him?"

"Technically, Eli does," Lucky informed her as they
came in sight of the house. "Bought him when we decided to quit the circuit."

"Why?"

"He didn't want to see the old guy go to the
slaughterhouse. Figured he had a few breeding years
left in him."

"Is that what the music was for?" JoJo asked,
wondering if a suggestive melody could affect an animal's hormones. "To get him in the mood?"

Maybe that's what was affecting her...having heard
the music. At least she hoped so.

"What music?"

"From the show."

Lucky sounded downright exasperated when he said, "You're talking in circles."

"The boombox in the pen—it was playing the rumba from the show at the Caribbean."

"Boombox?" Lucky's rugged features pulled into a harsh frown. "The Caribbean?"

But before he could question her further, a woman's voice echoed his. "What's this about the Caribbean?"

A female voice that JoJo wished she didn't recognize—that to her had the same effect as fingernails scraping over a blackboard.

"Caroline," she returned.

Her flat tone indicated her lack of enthusiasm at seeing her least favorite Donatelli sibling. She glanced at Lucky. No surprise crossed his features.

"I thought you were going to shower or something," he said.

"I chose the *or something*," Caroline stated, her glittering green eyes raking over JoJo, still held tight in Lucky's embrace.

Any doubts that she'd had about Lucky's identity vanished. And obviously, brother and sister had caught up with one another while she was out walking...or while she was playing keep-away with a Brahma bull.

"So what on earth is going on here?" Caroline continued. "You couldn't snare one brother, so now you're going after the other?"

"Comforting that some things never change, I guess," JoJo muttered. Caroline was being her usual charming self.

Lucky finally set her down, though he kept an arm around her waist until she wriggled free. "I take it you two ladies know each other."

"Not only am I acquainted with this *hussy,* but I know her type," Caroline said, moving in to take her brother's arm possessively. "And so do you, Lucky. All too well."

Her intimation being that he should be smart enough to stay away from her, JoJo realized, fuming.

"What brings *you* here, Caroline?" Out of sorts—who wouldn't be after being bull bait and then man-handled?—she couldn't help adding, "Didn't Daddy give you enough work to keep you busy?"

Caroline's stunning features hardened, and JoJo knew she'd hit a nerve. The other woman wanted Sally to see her as his equal, to make her his partner and the heir apparent to handle his empire. Sally felt the "family business" needed a man's hand, and to that end, he was constantly trying to suck Nick back into working with him.

"Papa always gives me plenty to do. That's why I needed a little rest," Caroline said, her voice cold. "Imagine my surprise when I arrived here and saw my recalcitrant baby brother...not to mention *you.*"

Lucky didn't look like anyone's baby brother, headstrong or otherwise, but for some reason he tolerated Caroline's name-calling. As a matter of fact, he appeared amused by their verbal sparring. JoJo glared at him and started off, meaning to go past him, toward the sanctuary of the house and her room, until he put out an arm to stop her.

"Not so fast. Let's get back to Bushwhacker."

She stood her ground. "I'd rather not. Once around the dance floor with that old bull was more than enough for me, thank you so much."

"Luckily, he didn't step on your toes."

"Or anything else."

Not one to be left out of a conversation, Caroline asked her brother, "Who's Bushwhacker?"

Lucky ignored her. "You're sure someone left a boombox in the pen?"

"Trust me on this one."

"And you said something about music from the show at the Caribbean."

"That's what it was playing. Actually, to be exact, the rumba that I dance to."

"Why would someone around here choose that music?" It was more of a question than an accusation. "And why would anyone leave a boombox in the middle of a bull enclosure?"

"That's what I was trying to find out."

"Bushwhacker could have hurt himself!"

"Himself? What about me?"

"I get the feeling you know how to take care of yourself...no matter what."

Furious, JoJo tore her gaze from him. Caroline seemed no more sympathetic. The other woman didn't even register surprise. Her expression was closed. And as cold as JoJo knew her capable of being.

Seeming not to notice, Lucky cocked his hat back on his head. "I'd better get that contraption out of the enclosure before the noise drives Bushwhacker nuts."

"You're a little late," JoJo informed him. "He took care of the problem himself. All that's left of the boombox is a hunk of twisted metal. But I guess you'd better make sure he didn't hurt *himself*," she added sarcastically.

"I'll do that."

He was obviously more anxious for the bull's well-being than hers. Though he'd carried her back to the house, JoJo saw the gesture as Lucky's sneaky way of imposing his will *over* her rather than as one of concern *for* her. She gave both Donatelli siblings a cold shoulder and headed for her room. A shower would revitalize her, as would another trip to town. Maybe she could lose herself in the art galleries.

And this time, she had no intention of coming back for dinner.

"WHERE DID that infernal woman get herself to now?" Lucky muttered irritably when the guests gathered for dinner in the dining area and he realized JoJo hadn't even returned to the ranch.

While Adair and Paula and Rocky took seats at the table, he hung back, pacing before the fireplace. Placing a platter of fried chicken on the table, Flora looked at him questioningly, but he held out a hand and shook his head. Caroline remained seated on a couch, watching him, undoubtedly wondering at his interest.

Lucky wondered himself.

"She probably decided to eat in town," Caroline said. "So what's the big deal?"

"Just want to keep my eye on her," Lucky hedged.

He wasn't about to share his mixed feelings for the woman with his sister. He'd found the boombox, all right, though the unmarked tape inside had been smashed to smithereens so he couldn't check it out. Had someone set JoJo up to be hurt for some reason? Or was JoJo working some kind of a con on him? Maybe she was trying to get his sympathy so she could get closer to him. If so, he could let her get closer, all right. He could beat her at her own game with his eyes closed and one hand tied behind his back.

"I don't trust her," he muttered.

"Good. No reason you should."

He eyed Caroline, remembered how overprotective she'd become of him and Nick after their mother had died and their father had been incarcerated. In some ways, Caroline, the middle child, had taken on the responsibility of their missing parents. She'd grown up the fastest, had lost the best years of her childhood. He loved her for the sacrifice, but he also knew her failings. The unnatural sense of responsibility had warped her judgment when it came to her brothers. No woman had ever been good enough for either him or Nick.

Coincidentally, so far, she'd been right, at least as far as he knew. . . .

"You don't like JoJo."

He kept his voice low so the guests wouldn't hear. Not that they were paying attention to him. They were too busy passing around platters of Flora's food and talking about taking a long ride the next morning. Earlier, he'd heard Paula tell Adair that she and Rocky had never gotten themselves horses because they hadn't been able to find Vincent—something he'd have to check out first thing in the morning. It was time he started asserting himself around the place.

"No, I don't like JoJo," Caroline agreed, also in a low voice. "She's trouble. Has been from the moment she arrived in Vegas."

"Nick obviously likes her."

"Nick is blind when it comes to women."

Lucky didn't remember his older brother having that particular failing...except for his fascination with Mia Scudella. Nick had fallen for the daughter of another crime boss, Salvatore Donatelli's chief rival. Carmine Scudella had lusted after Sally's territory and had seen his opportunity to take over while his rival was behind bars. Mia had been using Nick on her father's orders, had even gotten herself engaged to him. Luckily for Nick, she hadn't gone through with the marriage, but had broken it off. Unluckily for Mia, she'd been murdered shortly afterward.

"So Nick did have a fling with JoJo?" he asked.

Caroline's gaze flicked away, to the painting of Cathedral Rock over the fireplace. "Until someone else interested her more. Marco Scudella."

He started at the mention of Mia's twin brother. "What?" he bellowed.

And the conversation at the table came to a dead halt. Lucky felt four pairs of eyes turn toward him, including Flora's. "No problem," he told them. "Enjoy your dinners." Then to Caroline, he said, "Let's take it outside."

She rose and followed him onto the front porch, seemingly eager to give him all the details. "JoJo and Marco were secretly engaged. He was just out of prison and using an alias. And she was feeding him information about Nick. Marco blamed Nick for Mia's death and was determined to get even with him. Anyway, it's a long story, but suffice it to say that JoJo would be married to Marco now if he weren't in jail, awaiting trial for murdering a show girl."

JoJo and Marco. The thought twisted his gut good. Not that he'd had any dealings with the adult Marco.

Carmine's son had done hard time starting as a teenager and had been out of circulation for years. But Lucky remembered Marco as a kid, a mean little bastard, slippery as a snake when it came to covering his butt. As far as he was concerned, snakes might change their skins, but not their nature.

And JoJo had been engaged to him?

"So, if Nick found out JoJo was tight with a Scudella, why didn't he tell her to go to hell?" Lucky asked, a sour taste in his mouth.

Caroline ducked her head, hiding her expression. "Because she's his new wife's best friend."

"Right." She'd told him Nick was married now, a foreign concept as far as Lucky was concerned. "So he's tolerating her for his bride's sake. But why send her here?"

"Actually, it was Papa's idea," Caroline said. "The whole thing was arranged at the last minute. I had no idea until I was ready to leave and he told me she'd be here."

Though he remembered her pretending surprise upon seeing JoJo, Lucky didn't challenge his sister. He was too preoccupied mulling over his original assumption. "Then I was right." His father was as capable of using people as Carmine and Marco were. That JoJo had been in love with a Scudella undoubtedly meant little to him in the grander scheme of things. "She is working for Papa."

He looked to Caroline for confirmation. Her expression odd, she merely shrugged, as if she didn't know. But Lucky had no doubts she would do anything for their father, because family loyalty was everything to her. Was she in on the plan with the old man and not liking it?

"I've gotta find her."

He flew off the porch, but Caroline caught up to him near his Bronco. She grabbed his arm and stopped him. "Lucky, just leave her be."

"Don't stick your nose where it doesn't belong, Caroline!"

"Why, because I don't count? Don't I mean anything to you?"

Emotions had always stuck in Lucky's craw. He had a hard time putting words to them. "You're my sister."

"Not so that anyone would know it."

Here it came, the accusations that he'd seen in Caroline's eyes earlier when she'd arrived and had come face-to-face with him for the first time in six years. Hurt that she'd swallowed when she'd thrown her arms around him and told him how glad she was to see him. Guilt shot through Lucky. He'd meant to punish his father, not Nick or Caroline.

Now tears shone in her green eyes. "You disappeared, damn it! You never once wrote. You never once called. You could have been dead, for all we knew!"

Her hearing his reasons wouldn't make her feel any better. "I may be a little worse for the wear, but I'm alive, as you can see."

"And that's all you're going to say on the subject?" she asked, her voice rising.

"For now. First, I've got other things to take care of."

Exasperation marred her perfect features. "Going after that woman? What's the point?"

"The point is that no one messes with Lucky Donatelli without getting messed back!"

Anger turning to caution, a wide-eyed Caroline blinked and took a step away from him...almost as if she were suddenly afraid.

"Do what you have to do," she whispered.

Lucky did. He climbed into his Bronco and sped off, determined to find JoJo Weston and give her as good as she deserved. He'd make peace with his sister later.

Though Sedona was a small town, the shops, art galleries and restaurants were spread out along a couple of roads, one leading to the mouth of Oak Creek Canyon. As he dodged tourists, Lucky searched the street for JoJo's vehicle, but the only red Cherokee he spotted had Arizona license plates. After passing the last building with no luck, he turned his Bronco around and headed back onto the less populated strip along the highway.

Mouth set in a grim line, he searched every parking lot of every restaurant or coffee shop along the way, the conversation with his sister fueling his irritability when he didn't find her truck. He didn't expect to see it sitting outside of Sedona Sam's, a weather-beaten frame building with a big glowing red neon sign.

Though he hadn't been inside in years, he remembered the joint as being little better than a watering hole, though it used to serve good sandwiches and better steaks. Nothing fancy about the place that undoubtedly still catered to locals rather than tourists, that was for sure. But it was exactly right for his purposes.

Lucky was ready to do whatever was necessary to get JoJo Weston off his neck...and off his property for good.

JOJO LEANED BACK in the rough-hewn wooden booth, tapping her nails against her beer mug to the beat of the country music blasting from the jukebox. She'd spent the whole afternoon wandering from one art gallery to another. Satiated with all decorative things Western, she was glad to be in an unpretentious place free of the tourist hordes she'd been experiencing all day.

At least window-shopping had taken her mind off her encounter with the bull for several hours.

Again, thinking how close she'd come to getting hurt, JoJo felt a tremor shoot through her. She hadn't considered a visit to a real working ranch held its own brand of danger. Now she was forewarned and would be extra careful about poking her nose where it didn't belong. That what happened might not have been an accident occurred to her, but she couldn't accept the fact. She didn't want to think any deeper about the incident, didn't need any more stress in her life.

But suddenly, stress turned up like a bad penny.

"Give me whatever you have on draft and the biggest steak you can rustle up," boomed a familiar male voice.

JoJo's heart raced, whether from aggravation or excitement she wasn't certain. Standing between the bar and a handful of tables that were mostly empty, Lucky Donatelli loomed over the middle-aged blond waitress who scribbled his order on her pad. He was still wearing those butt-hugging jeans, but he'd pulled a chambray work shirt over the white T-shirt. Not that a long-sleeved shirt took anything away from him.

"How you want that steak done?" the waitress asked.

"Still bleeding." He was looking JoJo's way when he said it. "And I'll be waiting for my order over there, in that booth with the little redhead."

Little, her Aunt Fanny. JoJo decided aggravation was definitely in order and tried to work up a good case as he crossed to her booth, trying to hide his limp.

Lucky slid into the bench opposite her. "Drinking alone again, are you?"

"Not that it's any of your business—this is merely a lite beer and I'm waiting for a steak sandwich." JoJo looked at him pointedly. "What are *you* doing here?"

"Would you believe coincidence?"

"No."

"Smart lady. How smart?"

She considered the question for a moment. "I have a feeling there is no safe answer."

He stared at her from hooded eyes, as if he were looking through her. "Not bad."

JoJo's skin crawled. What was that supposed to mean? And what was he up to?

Staring at his belt buckle engraved with a bull, rider and some writing, she said, "I have a feeling *you're* not safe."

"Smarter than I thought."

Before she could demand he explain himself—demand to know why he followed her—the waitress interrupted.

"Here you go." She set a beer down in front of Lucky, then turned to JoJo. "Your sandwich is just coming up, honey. You want me to hold it until your friend's steak is done?"

"My *friend* wasn't invited." And JoJo's stomach was growling. She hadn't eaten since breakfast. "I'll have that sandwich now, thanks."

"Okay." The waitress rushed off toward the kitchen.

Lucky's expression didn't even change when he said, "That wasn't very sociable of you."

"I'm not feeling very sociable." As usual, she was on edge with him, the reason she'd stayed away from the ranch all day. One of them, she amended, Caroline being another. Now here he was anyway. "I'm hungry."

"I like a woman with an appetite."

"What do you want, Lucky?"

"A private confab."

"I'm not in the mood for another of our little chats." Somehow, he always got to her.

"I'm willing to make your job easier."

"What job?" she asked, following the question with a slug of beer.

"Getting close to me."

She nearly choked out the mouthful of liquid, but somehow managed a save. Swallowing hard, she said, "Come again?" directly in the face of his devilish grin.

"Here you go, honey." A plate plunked down before her. "Another beer?"

Stunned by Lucky's arrogant statement, she muttered, "Uh, I'm not done with this one yet."

"Catch you in a few."

The moment the waitress was out of hearing range, JoJo turned back to Lucky, her gaze steely. "Now, what was that you said about getting close to you?"

Expression guileless, he insisted, "Later, on full stomachs," and took refuge in his own brew.

Considering her steak sandwich as if it were Lucky's flesh, JoJo bit into the beef with a savagery that was oddly satisfying. Mouth full, she glared at him, wondering if he was making it his life's work to torture her, or if he was merely the most hostile man she'd ever met.

"So you don't believe in coincidences?" he asked.

Still working on the mouthful of food, she shook her head and made a negative sound.

"Neither do I." He sprawled back in his booth, staring at her steadily, as if looking for a reaction when he said, "I'm referring to the Bushwhacker incident."

JoJo swallowed. "What about it?"

"Eli takes care of the old bull himself. I asked him about the boombox. First he'd heard of it."

"What about Vincent?"

"Vincent didn't seem to be around this morning. At least that's what Paula said when she and Rocky couldn't find him to get those horses."

"Maybe that's because he was working in the enclosure."

"Maybe. But working at what?"

"I just thought...I don't know." She hadn't seen signs of any work in progress inside the pen, but then, she'd been otherwise occupied and hadn't exactly taken too close a look. "There must be some simple explanation."

Agitated, JoJo took another bite of her sandwich. For a moment, she thought Lucky was going to let the subject drop, but that turned out to be hopeful thinking.

"Let's see," he mused. "We have a boombox in an enclosure with an irritable old bull...a gate left open...you heading for the house right past that gate...a tape of music that's from a show at my brother's hotel...music that *you* dance to.'' He swigged some beer and nodded. ''Uh-huh. Must be a real simple explanation.''

JoJo suddenly lost her appetite. Lucky was making a weird incident out to be more than she was comfortable with. He was either intimating that she'd pulled the stunt herself...or that someone had wanted to see her hurt. She didn't like either conclusion. She figured he believed the first. She didn't want to believe the second. Buried beneath her self-assurances, the nasty suspicion that trouble had followed her from Las Vegas had plagued her, but she'd put it off to her nerves, to sheer imagination.

She'd been similarly dismissive of whatever had spooked Spitfire the day before.

Those noises *had* sounded like gunshots, she remembered, whether or not they'd actually been aimed at her.

JoJo was shaking inside and trying to look normal. She didn't want Lucky to see how much his taunting bothered her. She didn't want him to smell her fear.

For she was afraid. Of what had happened to her with Marco and Lester. Of the way it had affected her, unsettled her mind. But most of all, she was afraid of Lucky.

From the moment they'd clashed, he'd made no bones about wanting her off his land. She'd defied him by staying. She'd angered him...and she didn't know what he was capable of. He wasn't like Nick. He wasn't even like Caroline. He was an unknown quantity, a man with a blank past.

He could be anything.

Could have done anything.

Could be willing to do anything to get rid of her.

Chapter Five

JoJo meant to keep Lucky's obscure past and possible threat to her in mind. Somehow, she managed to force another swallow of food past the lump in her throat. The task looked to be a bit easier when his steak arrived—chewing would keep his mouth busy doing something other than continuing to put the fear of God in her.

"You ready for that second beer?" the waitress asked her.

"Sure. Keep it lite."

Lucky pushed his empty mug toward the blonde, as well. "Fill it up with premium."

Thankfully, Lucky made no further reference to the "Bushwhacker incident," as he'd called it. But the implication lay before JoJo like a tangible thing. She played with a French fry, breaking the potato stick into bits. If Lucky noticed, it didn't give him pause. He began wolfing down his steak as if he hadn't eaten in days.

Would Lucky Donatelli actually have planted the seeds of doubt in her mind if he'd been the one responsible for luring her into a dangerous situation?

Then again, he had been conveniently handy to catch her escaping over the fence.

Hmm. Guilt by proximity?

She didn't think the accusation would wash. And she hadn't actually been hurt. Besides, he'd been close enough to "save" her if necessary. Maybe he'd merely wanted her to be scared enough to run back to Las Vegas.

But why?

JoJo realized Lucky had expected to have the run of the property. He and Eli. What if they were up to something they didn't want anyone else to know about?

"You certainly have a healthy appetite," she said when he continued eating nonstop. "What have you been doing all day?"

"I managed to keep busy."

"With Eli?"

"We had things to do," he agreed.

"Around the ranch?"

"Mmph."

The noncommittal sound could mean anything. JoJo took another bite of her sandwich. Fat chance that he and Eli could carry through some secret plot now. He had not only her to contend with, but three other unforeseen guests, not to mention his sister.

Caroline!

Suddenly it occurred to JoJo that not only had Lucky been in the vicinity of the enclosure right after the episode, but so had his sister, and she'd shown up unexpectedly, too. Caroline never had made any bones about her antipathy for the women Nick dated and though JoJo and Nick had merely been friends, she'd been no exception. Caroline had been nearby when

Nick had offered her the stay at the ranch. And as the sister of the owner, she probably had access to a recording of music from the Caribbean's show, as well.

JoJo wouldn't put it past Caroline to play a nasty trick on her. Maybe it had something to do with Sasha's marrying Nick. Her best friend never would have left New York City if not for her.

And maybe Lucky was innocent of wrongdoing, after all.

Relaxing her guard a little, JoJo allowed herself to eat, if not actually enjoy, the rest of her sandwich and half of the second beer. Then she sat back to study Lucky, who was in the process of cleaning his plate.

"Are you really done with the rodeo circuit?" she asked.

"I never said."

"Well, are you?"

"Could be."

"Depending on . . . ?"

"On whether or not some plans I have work out."

Had she nailed it or what? JoJo tried not to let her triumph show. "What kind of plans?"

"Not ready to talk about them."

"Not even with Eli?"

"Eli's involved."

"So secretive."

"So nosy."

Not the first time he'd said so. Again the nagging suspicion that he'd counted on her inquisitiveness to lure her into the enclosure.

"Nothing wrong with a little curiosity, is there?" JoJo asked, lifting her mug.

Lucky sat back, his agate eyes trying to bore a hole through her. "I guess not . . . even if it's about Marco Scudella, right?"

At the abrupt change of subject, JoJo nearly choked on her beer, her involvement with Marco being the last topic she'd expected him to bring up.

"How do you know about Marco?" Then it came to her. "What am I thinking? Of course...Caroline."

"She said you were engaged to him."

"Did she?"

"Engagement still on?"

She'd never formally told Mac, alias Marco, to go where the sun didn't shine, but that merely had been an oversight, a fact that didn't concern Lucky.

"What's it to you?"

It took him a tad too long to say "Nothing. Just a little curiosity. Or does that curiosity thing being okay only apply to you?"

"You haven't been forthcoming about anything, so stuff it."

Not wanting to get further into the subject with a virtual stranger, JoJo was relieved that the waitress chose that moment to appear.

The blonde started clearing plates and asked, "Anything else?"

"My check," JoJo said.

"You can give it to me," Lucky offered.

"Give him everything he deserves," JoJo said, "but I intend to pay my own way."

The blonde's eyebrows shot up. "Whatever."

Setting down the dishes on a nearby tray, the waitress scribbled on her pad and tore off two checks. JoJo wasted no time settling her bill, leaving an overly generous tip rather than having to wait for change.

"Have a good one," JoJo told Lucky as she shot out of the booth and out of the establishment.

The parking lot was dark but for the neon sign that cast a reddish glow over everything in its path. She'd hardly set foot on the pavement before Lucky caught up to her.

"What's the rush?" he asked, trying not to limp.

"I walk fast." She dug her keys from her pocket. "Long legs."

"So I noticed." He was noticing now, his eyes seemingly glued to them, even in the near-dark. "We have some unfinished business."

A warning shot through her. "I don't think so."

Despite her protest, Lucky headed her off, cut between her and the Cherokee. He took the key ring from her, unlocked and opened the driver's door. She held out her hand, expecting to get the keys back. Ignoring the silent demand, Lucky twirled the ring around a finger, jangling metal against metal, as if daring her to go for it.

Tension stretched between them. JoJo considered her options. She wasn't about to give Lucky the satisfaction of contact sport, no matter that the thought set fire to her imagination. Only because she wasn't going anywhere without those keys did she finally give in.

"All right. What exactly do you want to talk about?"

"The reason you're here."

She chose to take him literally. "I'm here because you won't let me leave."

"At the ranch."

"It's called a vacation."

"You said you didn't believe in coincidence."

Were they back to Bushwhacker? "I don't."

"Then why did you arrive on Macbride property a half-dozen hours after I did? Just long enough to pack a couple of bags and drive down from Las Vegas?"

Now she was lost. "I don't get the significance."

"You've got great moves," he said, moving in on her, making her catch her breath. "All the earmarks of Sally Donatelli trying to figure an angle on getting his wayward son back into the family business. I'm sure he figured I couldn't resist you if you tried hard enough, that you could lead me back into the fold."

Slowly, through a haze of warmth dancing along her nerves, it dawned on her. "You think I'm doing your father some kind of favor?"

His voice was low—menacing?—when he said, "More like working for him."

She licked her lips and backed up toward her vehicle. "I work for your brother."

"Show girls don't make squat."

"I make enough to get along," she said defensively, trying to work up some natural outrage... trying to break the connection that should be ticking her off.

"But you'd like more, wouldn't you?"

Who wouldn't? But she wasn't willing to prostitute herself to get more. Figuring he'd met plenty of women who might, she tried to remain calm. She had to consider the source.

"You're way off base."

"Am I?"

Lucky inched closer, his not-so-subtle physical threat making her heart race.

JoJo felt confused... scared... intrigued. On the one hand, she wanted to turn tail and run. Find someplace safe where Lucky couldn't find her. On the other, she wanted to challenge him, to see where it would take them. Yet, underlying the physical motivations, she wanted Lucky to recognize her integrity.

"The reason I accepted your brother's offer to stay at the ranch was because I needed some time to myself," she told him. "To mentally unwind."

"From what?"

"Personal reasons."

She didn't feel comfortable sharing the nightmare she'd gone through with a stranger...especially not one who was ready to think the worst of her. And who knew what exactly Caroline had already told him about her relationship with Marco? From the way Lucky seemed to remain unmoved, she sensed the truth fell on deaf ears.

"Tell me you haven't been running a number on me," he said.

"I haven't been running a number on you."

Again the truth. Any connection between them was real, at least as far as she was concerned. Despite his opinion, attraction was nearly overwhelming her. Blood pulsed through her body to her extremities, the tingling in her fingers urging her to reach out and touch him.

"What about last night?" he whispered.

Remembering how she'd been held fast when she'd wanted to go to her room—the same invisible tension tying her up in knots now—she asked, "What about it?"

"You gave me all the right signals."

Her blood pulsed in a rushing sound through her head, a sensation at once sensual and frightening.

"I wasn't coming on to you."

JoJo's eyes widened as Lucky came on to her so swiftly she couldn't think. One step and he pinned her back against the driver's seat. He was barely touching her, but heat coiled along her nerves. He raised his arms, hooking his hands on the roof of the vehicle.

Still, she envisioned them thigh to thigh, belly to belly, breasts to chest. And before she could do anything to shatter the fantasy, he made it real.

His head plunged. They made contact.

The rushing sound in her head blotted out any rational thought that might urge her to stop now, before it was too late. Acting on age-old instinct, she responded, opening her mouth, inviting him in.

Lucky explored her offering, nipping at the sensitive flesh just inside her lower lip, then deepening the kiss, his tongue plundering. JoJo arched her back away from the vehicle, her breasts flattening against his chest. A sound issued low in his throat, and his thigh somehow wedged its way between hers, its pulsing rhythm reminding her of sex.

Wet warmth flooded her, and all lucid thought fled. JoJo gave in to the moment. The sheer excitement. The ache unlike any she'd ever known building in her.

She slid her arms around Lucky's back, and dug her fingers into the heat of his flesh through the soft material of his shirt. She was floating, and yet her limbs were heavy, taking away her will to move them if she would.

Not that she had any such desire.

For a moment, Lucky might have done anything to her, might have convinced her to do anything to him.

Then suddenly, he broke the kiss and pulled back, giving her more than breathing room. Giving her space enough to come to her senses, to make her wonder what had just happened.

The red glow of neon illuminated Lucky's face, and JoJo went cold inside. If the kiss had affected him, she couldn't see it in the harsh features that glared at her. He looked like the very devil he was named for—Lucifer incarnate. She was certain he'd meant to prove something, to punish her with that kiss.

Embarrassment flooded her in sickening waves, and it took all JoJo's willpower to do nothing more damaging with the flat of her hand than hold it out when what she really wanted to do was smack him.

"My keys."

JoJo gazed at Lucky steadily and was rewarded with the key ring being slapped in her hand. Her fingers curled around the metal, and while the urge to flee was there, she did not immediately jump into the driver's seat. She'd been treated despicably by one man, and she'd never had the satisfaction of telling him what she thought of him. No way had she wanted to visit Marco in jail under any circumstances.

But Lucky was here, a captive audience, so to speak. And she would think less of herself if she let this go. If she let him think he had won in some way.

"I don't know what kind of numbers you've pulled on other women," she began, her voice sharp, "but I'm not them. Nor am I a woman who seduces men for favors or for pay. If you think you taught me some kind of lesson, think again. You might be his son, but you just proved that you don't have half the polish of Sally Donatelli."

JoJo took a bittersweet satisfaction in the further darkening of Lucky's visage. Part of her thought she should be afraid. But she was pumped, her adrenaline at an all-time high. And wanting to leave on a high note, she slid into the Cherokee and grabbed the door handle.

"You're in the way," she said bluntly.

His gaze glued to her, Lucky stepped back. A thrill of warning shot up her spine as she swung the door closed and started the engine. He still hadn't moved off when she pulled out of the parking spot and drove away.

Once on the highway, JoJo felt her adrenaline plunge, leaving her body limp and trembling. Her hands were shaking, too. Wondering if she were crazy to antagonize a man who gave off every indication that he could be dangerous, she couldn't feel regret at her castigating him. He'd deserved everything she'd said and more.

What had Lucky been trying to prove anyway? Had the kiss been another attempt to scare her off, away from the ranch? Had he appeared so grim because she'd responded rather than running as he'd hoped?

She had to be crazy to want to stay, JoJo told herself, but the kiss that had been meaningless to him had reinforced her stubborn streak. The uncomfortable situation was becoming a test of wills, not exactly conducive to her mental health. Or to her physical well-being, either, she thought, remembering Lucky's speculation about the Bushwhacker incident.

Not that she'd actually been hurt, she reminded herself.

Not that she even knew anyone was trying to pull something on her, either.

But what if . . . ?

By the time she parked in front of the ranch house, JoJo was wondering if she shouldn't leave in the

morning, despite her mulish nature. Maybe this once
she should forget her damn pride and worry about her
skin. And when she found Caroline relaxing in front
of the fire, she figured retreating wasn't such a bad
thing if it meant she didn't have to deal with the Donatelli sister.

Cold green eyes assessed her. "JoJo. You finally
found your way back here."

"Disappointed?"

Caroline took a sip from a glass of wine. "Actually, I've been waiting for you."

"Don't bother," JoJo said wearily, about to an-
nounce the good news that she was leaving.

"But I feel it's my civic duty to warn you."

"About what?"

"Lester Perkins, of course."

JoJo started. "Something happened to Lester?"
Despite herself, she moved closer to the other woman.

"I'm afraid so."

Caroline was drawing out her announcement, was
enjoying making her sweat, JoJo realized. "I'm too
tired to play out this little—"

"Lester Perkins is on the loose."

JoJo's heart threatened to stop... then went wild.
"You're joking, right?"

"Afraid not." Caroline appeared perfectly serious,
even a bit worried, when she explained. "He escaped
before dawn the morning of the wedding."

Legs shaking, JoJo sat. She'd seen him. Dear Lord,
she'd seen him in the crowd and she'd thought her
imagination was playing tricks on her. She hadn't been
imagining anything. Lester Perkins was on the loose.

"How did you find out?"

"When they hadn't tracked Lester down by the next day, someone in the sheriff's office called the Caribbean to warn Nick. Vito took the call."

"They think Lester's dangerous?"

Caroline gave her a look. "You, of all people, should know just how dangerous."

"But Lester never tried to hurt me."

"Excuse me? He kidnapped you."

"He was protecting me from Marco."

"In his own twisted mind, maybe. And what did he get for his trouble? A tour in the psych ward." Caroline's gaze was frank rather than malicious when she added, "I doubt that Lester views you with the same slavelike devotion that he used to."

Because Lester Perkins had worked for her father before her brother, Caroline knew him better than JoJo did.

"You think he's out for revenge?" JoJo swallowed hard. "Against *me?*"

"He's not a very stable man. His helping you got him in trouble big time, and took him away from his predictable but secure life. What do you think?"

JoJo didn't know what to think other than to put her plans to head back to Las Vegas on hold for the moment. If Lester were running loose around town, she'd rather not be anywhere in his radius. Though she believed Caroline, she'd call the sheriff's department first thing in the morning to find out whether or not Lester was still at large.

Until then . . .

"I think I'd better get some sleep," JoJo finally said, rising.

Caroline raised her wineglass. "Happy dreams."

For once, JoJo thought the other woman was sincere, maybe even felt sorry for her.

If only she didn't have reason to.

VISIONS OF THE MOUSY maintenance man dancing in her head, JoJo barely slept at all, and when she rose, the first thing she did after getting dressed was to place the phone call that plunged her back into the nightmare she'd hoped was over.

"Sorry, Miss Weston, but Lester Perkins is still at large," Deputy Sheriff Ben Carter told her.

JoJo gripped the cordless phone. "How did he get away in the first place?"

"That matter is still under investigation. I'm not at liberty to speculate."

"I see." She stared into the now-cold fireplace, thinking her life was suddenly in ashes, too. "Why didn't you inform me when this happened?"

"Someone was instructed to call all the people involved in the Perkins case, Miss Weston. I guess you weren't home. You don't have an answering machine?"

"My answering machine. Of course. I'm afraid I haven't thought to call my home number to get my messages the last couple of days."

"Then you're out of town?"

"In Arizona. The Macbride Ranch near Sedona."

"Good. That takes you out of the picture as a target."

A target.

Boy, was she ever beginning to feel like one. JoJo wasn't certain which would be worse—staying here and trying to avoid any more accidents or going home and trying to avoid Lester, who might even now be looking for her. Great choice. At home she would be alone, no one to turn to if she did get into trouble. Here she would have more company than she needed.

In the end, she had no choice at all, JoJo realized. And if Lucky didn't like her continuing presence, he would just have to lump it.

"I'll be here for at least a few more days," she told the deputy. "Would you please call me the moment you know anything more?"

"Yes, ma'am, we'll do that," he assured her.

She gave Deputy Carter the ranch's number and switched off the phone for a moment as memories swamped her.

Being tricked into what would be her dungeon for a week...Lester's assuring her that he was going to keep her away from her prospective groom for her own good...being alone in the near-dark, hour upon hour, each day wondering whether Lester would come back or leave her to rot in that dank room in the theater's subbasement.

Giving herself a shake—nothing like that could happen to her here—JoJo decided to call home and pick up her messages. There were three. The first was indeed from the sheriff's department. The second was from Sasha checking to make certain JoJo had left town as promised. The third was from a woman with a familiar-sounding East Coast accent.

"Miss Weston, this is Marva Levine from the law firm of Abrams and Horowitz in New York. Since we haven't heard from you, I fear you didn't receive our letter. Could you please return my call at your convenience? The number is 212-555-3647. I'll be looking forward to hearing from you."

Clicking off, JoJo frowned. She'd received the letter informing her of Oliver's death, all right, but she didn't remember a request to call the law firm. Then again, she'd been so upset, she hadn't actually read the missive all the way through.

Thinking she ought to do so, she rose just as Paula Gibson breezed into the living room.

"Morning, JoJo!" she called cheerily. "Want to join us for a trail ride this morning after breakfast?"

"Who's us?"

"Rocky and me. Someone told Rocky a movie company was just shooting at this ghost town less than an hour's ride from here, and we thought it would be a hoot to check it out."

This must be the movie Adair Keating had been working on. The ride would get her away from the ranch for a while, and with a couple of companions, JoJo realized. And she had to admit there would be safety in numbers.

"Sure. It'll be fun."

Fresh air and open spaces were just the things she needed to rid herself of the claustrophobic atmosphere created by her memories.

"Great!" Paula enthused. "I hope Lucky had that talk with Vincent Zamora, though."

"About what?"

"About disappearing like he did yesterday." Paula hooked her hair behind her ear. "We couldn't find him to get us horses, so we were stuck around here all morning. We finally gave up and drove into town."

Remembering she'd originally thought Vincent had been playing the rumba music while he was working around the place, JoJo wondered where the ranch hand had gone off to. It was odd that he would have done a disappearing act at the very time she'd gotten herself into trouble.

Now she was fabricating. There was no reason to think the wrangler had anything against her.

First Lucky, then Caroline, now Vincent...

Still, when Flora arrived and began breakfast, and Paula left to find Vincent and ask him to saddle up some horses, JoJo found herself alone with the housekeeper for a while. So she decided to see what she could find out about the man.

"Has Vincent Zamora worked for the ranch long?" JoJo asked, carrying a stack of plates to the table.

"A few months only."

"Then you don't know him very well." She went back for the cups and saucers. "I mean what kind of a person he is."

An odd expression crossed Flora's features. "He's a wild card, that one."

"Why do you say that? I ask because he makes me uncomfortable." When she feared the housekeeper wouldn't be forthcoming, JoJo added, "I'm not a paying guest. I'm a friend of Nick's, remember."

Flora shook her head. "He's the wrong man to work with guests. I don't know what Henry was thinking. He should've taken Vincent on the range to round up strays and left someone else behind." She took a big breath and in a low voice added, "Vincent's been in jail a couple of times, and he's got a reputation for hiring himself out for trouble."

Paula and Rocky appeared before JoJo could delve further into the reasons. At least she knew enough to be wary around the wrangler if not enough to know why.

JoJo Weston was proving to be more trouble than initially anticipated.

Using the bull to do a job on her had been a stroke of genius. The circumstances had been perfect. She'd been alone with no one to save her. If all had gone as planned, she would be dead now....

But the show girl had outsmarted the crafty old bull. She'd bushwhacked Bushwhacker!

Somehow, she'd managed to save herself.

The challenge she presented might almost be amusing if so much weren't at stake. It was no time to play games. She had to be dispatched as quickly as possible, although having so many people around made the task more difficult. Still, she had to be punished in a very final way.

Then she couldn't go on fooling men, making them think they were special.

Where men were concerned, JoJo Weston was a liar.

A manipulator.

A cheat.

And the little schemer wasn't going to get the chance to work her wiles on another unsuspecting victim.

Chapter Six

Vincent Zamora wasn't the only man JoJo had to be wary of that morning. Having shown up alone halfway through breakfast and in the midst of the conversation about the trail ride, Lucky had insisted on coming along. That brought the group's number to five, since Adair Keating had already opted to join the other guests.

At least Caroline chose to absent herself from the group—a bit of a consolation, JoJo thought as she changed into her barely broken-in hand-tooled boots, stuffed her wallet into her rear jeans pocket and grabbed her cowboy hat.

When she ventured out of her bedroom, everyone was gathering near the door, eager to get started.

"Hey, finally a chance to step back into the Old West, where a man was a man," Rocky said, then pantomimed a quick draw with an imaginary gun. *"Bam!"*

He shot Adair, who obligingly caught himself around the middle and swayed as if he were ready to hit the dust.

"No firearms in the house," Lucky said dryly as he led the way out the front door. "Cowboys used to leave their holsters on pegs outside the front door."

"That's as bad as keeping an unloaded gun in your nightstand," Rocky complained. "What's the point of having it at all if you can't use it when you need it?"

Not wanting to get into a discussion about guns, which she personally hated, JoJo let the men go ahead and hung to the back of the pack with Paula. Still, she noticed Lucky's limp was hardly noticeable this morning.

"Isn't this exciting?" the other woman whispered as they headed for the pasture where Vincent would already have begun to tack up the horses. "Two of us and three of them?"

Divorced a few weeks, and Paula was already looking for a man. JoJo shrugged. Each to her own. At least Paula wasn't sitting at home feeling sorry for herself.

"Thrilling," JoJo replied, staring daggers at Lucky's back.

As if he could feel their sharpness, Lucky glanced over his shoulder at her. Even though she was unable to see his eyes because of the cowboy hat pulled low on his forehead, JoJo sensed them on her and immediately grew warm. She was glad when his attention was drawn back to the conversation with Rocky and Adair.

Since Vincent had only known about three riders, the group had to wait a few minutes while he tacked up a fourth horse, while Lucky got his own. The moment the Appaloosa spotted him, he trotted straight to Lucky.

"Hey, Silverado, how you doin', boy?" he asked, rubbing the horse's nose.

JoJo couldn't help but admire his ease with the animal and the apparent affection between man and beast that had to have come with time. She wondered if Lucky had brought his personal mount with him around the rodeo circuit, or if he'd bought Silverado somewhere along the way as Eli had Bushwhacker. Truthful with herself, she couldn't help admiring Lucky's strength as he tacked up the horse, the way his jeans and cotton shirt stretched over pure muscle. That part of him was definitely attractive.

Too bad he couldn't get a personality transplant...

"So what are you going to do while you're here?" Paula interrupted her private reflections. "I mean for the next couple of days."

"Chill out, mostly."

"Then have you thought about taking one of the vortex tours? You know—a guide takes you around to different sites in the red rocks. You're supposed to meditate, develop your spiritual side." Without waiting for JoJo's answer, Paula continued her chattering. "Or if you don't want to take an official tour, you and I could explore by ourselves. I have a book that explains everything. I believe in being prepared."

Surprised that the other woman seemed so interested in the metaphysical, not to mention in doing something with another woman rather than one of the men, JoJo said, "I'll give it some thought."

"Or we could gallery hop together if you prefer," Paula enthused. "I'm always on the lookout for silver pieces designed by Sadie Buckthorn."

Paula held out her right hand, today her long nails were painted canyon red. Her ring really was quite an interesting design, a combination of handworked sil-

ver and purple stone, that must have cost a small fortune.

"Beautiful," JoJo said. "But I think I've had all
the galleries I can take for a while." Noting Paula's
crestfallen expression, she added, "But we'll do
something together, I promise."

The other woman's lips curved in satisfaction.
"Great! Oh, I think we're ready."

JoJo looked around to find Vincent leading all four
horses toward them . . . and staring straight at *her*.

"Ready to mount up?" he asked.

"I'll stick with Spitfire."

"Figured." Vincent handed over the reins to the
chestnut mare. "You and her must have hit it off,
huh?"

"She has some spirit. We understand each other."

He leered at her, if a bit more discreetly than he had
the other day. "I just bet you do."

And even as she realized she was the center of
Lucky's attention, as well, he snapped, "Get the other
guests their horses, Zamora." He gave a hard tug on
his saddle's cinch as if for emphasis. "We want to get
out on the trail now. Rain's coming early this afternoon."

JoJo wondered if his clipped tone were meant for
the wrangler . . . or for her.

So far, though he'd done a few inspection tours of
her that morning, Lucky had avoided speaking directly to JoJo, irritating her as much as if he'd made
one of his hostile remarks. She checked the sky, a
brilliant blue against the deep greens of growth and
reds of sandstone in the distance. Not a cloud marred
its perfection. No sign of rain as far as she could tell.
She wondered if his weather prediction had been the

truth, or if Lucky had used the excuse to cover his impatience.

"You must be psychic," JoJo murmured as Spitfire danced toward Lucky and his mount. "About the rain coming."

"Not psychic. Just clever enough to get a weather report before going out into the desert." He swung up into his saddle, the smooth movement mesmerizing JoJo for a moment. "Maybe you haven't lived in the Southwest long enough to know how fickle—and *dangerous*—weather can be out here."

Under the impression that it didn't rain all that much in Arizona, which was known for its sunny days, JoJo said, "You wouldn't be trying to scare me, now, would you?" Another ploy to make her leave?

"This area is loaded with canyons and arroyos. When rain hits, it hits hard. Haven't you seen the flash-flood warnings wherever the land dips?"

JoJo shifted in her saddle, making Spitfire prance under her. "I guess I hadn't noticed."

A bit chagrined, she turned her attention to Vincent, who was introducing the guests to their horses. Flash, a bronze palomino with silvery mane and tail, for Paula. A black-and-white pinto named Apache for Rocky. And for Adair—Chocolate, a big dark bay.

When they were all mounted, Paula asked, "Could someone shorten these stirrups for me?"

Blue eyes wide, she was appealing directly to Lucky, who didn't seem to notice that she was flirting with him when he said, "Zamora, the lady needs an adjustment."

"Yes, sir!" Vincent tipped his hat to his new boss, though the gesture didn't exactly look congenial.

JoJo thought the stirrups seemed just the right length for Paula's legs, but the other woman wasn't satisfied until her knees were drawn up, as if she were used to an English saddle when she rode.

A moment later, they were on their way, Lucky taking the lead. JoJo noticed his horse's croup and hindquarters, gray decorated with black spots... and more than a few healed scars. She realized the rodeo circuit must be as tough on the animals as on the men who dared to ride them.

Lucky took them onto a trail opposite the one passing the apple orchard. Paula was next in line, followed by Rocky, and Adair brought up the rear behind JoJo. They'd barely stretched their horses' legs before Adair moved up next to her.

"You've done some riding in your time."

"Mostly on farm horses."

With the exception of Rocky Franzone, whose bottom *thump-thumped* in his saddle—and he was planning on working as a *wrangler?*—everyone appeared pretty comfortable, especially Paula. Her posture was perfect, if not for Western riding. She was shifted forward in the saddle, back straight, thighs and knees tight against the leather.

JoJo's impression that Paula normally rode English, unusual for someone who lived in Arizona, heightened. Then again, Paula had unusual and expensive interests...not to mention such unusually long nails that JoJo wondered how the secretary could possibly use a computer keyboard at her job. Maybe Paula had been supported in elegance while she was married. And JoJo suspected she wasn't the sort of woman who would give up nice nails for a job—she'd figure how to work around them.

Turning her attention back to Adair, JoJo asked, "Were you born on a horse, or did you get into it when you decided to be a stuntman?"

"I've done some riding here and there over the years," he said vaguely.

"So how much time did you spend in Rimrock?"

"Rimrock?"

"That's the name of the ghost town according to Flora. You were the one who told Rocky about it, right?"

"Not me."

"But you *were* doing stunts for *Call of the West* when the movie company was shooting there—"

"The name just never registered, I guess," he said, then suddenly dropped back behind her.

Why didn't Adair seem to want to talk about the experience? And why wouldn't he know the town's name?

How peculiar.

The country here was similar to that which she'd traversed the first time she went riding: rolling hills giving way to paths through sandstone rock. They skirted what looked like a small canyon, but they crossed one of the deep arroyos, or washes, Lucky had mentioned. At the moment, the earth that had been cut by fast-running water was bone-dry. Eventually they came to a gravel road and followed it a way, rounding a corner. The ghost town suddenly popped into view.

"There it is!" Paula said, moving her horse out of line and taking the lead.

Rocky and Adair followed, leaving Lucky and JoJo to bring up the rear. Lucky shortened his horse's stride until they were riding side by side. JoJo tensed, ready for a verbal shot of some kind, and so she was surprised when she glanced at him and he seemed relaxed.

"How about we start fresh?" Lucky asked. "It's obvious you're not going back to Las Vegas until you're good and ready, so we might as well try and get along."

She peered at him suspiciously. The brim of his hat continued to ride low, so his eyes remained shadowed and unreadable.

"Sounds like a reasonable suggestion," she said, her wariness warring with her relief.

"It's settled, then."

"As long as you don't make any more assumptions about me," she cautioned.

"I was merely acting on experience."

"Then in the future, you need to remember there are always exceptions to the rule."

"And you're one of them?"

She'd been known to go her own way, though she wasn't militant about it. "Depends on the rule."

His lips curved into what she thought of as a reluctant grin. "Fair enough warning."

Whatever that meant . . .

JoJo goosed Spitfire. As she played catch-up with the others, she was aware that Lucky took his time following. Too aware. But even with Lucky's peace offering, she couldn't totally relax around the man. She continually sensed his staring at her. Speculating about her. Giving her goose bumps when she least expected it.

Goose bumps best left for a ghost town, she thought wryly.

Rimrock consisted of a couple dozen ramshackle buildings, most with new false fronts, evidently provided by the movie company that had been shooting there.

"Isn't this fab?" Paula demanded, hanging on to her hat and twirling around in the middle of the dusty street. "Just like we stepped back in time."

JoJo dismounted, automatically checking her back pocket to make certain her wallet was secure.

"Where a man can be a man," she murmured with a snicker. Rocky was standing in the middle of the street, legs spread, hat pulled low, as though he were preparing for that gunfight at high noon. "I'm not certain I'd like being a woman who lived back then."

"Whyever not? There were tons of men for every woman. And you would probably have been a dance-hall girl, so you would have been very popular."

Paula didn't get it, and JoJo wasn't about to give her a diatribe on a woman having had disturbingly few rights in the last century. Dance-hall girl indeed. Undoubtedly, most of those poor young women were pressed into less appealing services for the men of the town.

She tied her horse's reins around a hitch in front of the general store as Lucky dismounted nearby.

"Be careful," he cautioned as the small group began to fan out. "These buildings are older than any of us. Could be rotted floorboards or beams inside. I don't want anyone hurt." He was looking at *her* when he said it. "It'd take some doing to get an ambulance out here."

The warning didn't dampen anyone's enthusiasm, though they all agreed to be careful. Adair stuck close to JoJo. And wherever she poked her nose, Lucky seemed to be in the general vicinity, as well, the feel of his steady gaze staying with her even when she left his line of sight. She didn't understand it. She'd only known the man for a couple of days, but Lucky continually crowded her thoughts. And despite the truce, her thoughts about him weren't all good ones, either.

"Hey, Adair, come look at this old saloon," Paula called.

"I've got plenty to look at over here."

"Stop being a poop and come on!"

Remembering Paula's interest in the men, JoJo grinned at him. "She won't leave you alone until you go."

With a sigh, Adair yelled, "I'm coming!" and set off across the rutted street.

Finding herself alone at last, JoJo wandered into a building designated Hayward's Stable by a freshly painted sign. The inside was dark but for the shaft of light coming from the hayloft above. The smell of fresh bales reminded her of her grandparents' farm and terrific memories of her growing-up years. Following the scent through the gloom across the hard-packed dirt floor, JoJo approached the ladder that would take her up to the hayloft.

She inspected several rungs. The ladder seemed perfectly safe, so she tested her way up to the base of the loft. It, too, was solid when she levered her weight on the edge before clambering across the straw-strewn surface, unquestionably a courtesy of the movie company.

JoJo made herself comfortable on a bale near the open doors, content to watch the activity below as her companions continued to explore the old ghost town. Paula. Rocky. Adair. Their voices echoed up to her.

Feeling more relaxed than she had since arriving at the ranch, she let her mind drift.

And darn if it didn't drift straight to Lucky Donatelli.

The son of a crime boss who had disappeared just before his father's incarceration was up. Nick had once told her that he, Caroline and Lucky had been working together to turn Sally's various interests legit. The Three Musketeers. So why hadn't Lucky stuck around to enjoy the fruits of his efforts? Why had he left his home to wander the West? And why had he changed from the happy-go-lucky guy Nick had told her about to this distrustful, cynical man?

Lucky was a puzzle if she'd ever met one. A puzzle she shouldn't concern herself with figuring out.

Sheer animal magnetism. No other explanation. She shifted uncomfortably as the kiss they'd shared came back to haunt her. The exploration. The building desire. The sheer heat of the moment.

And the dousing with cold reality afterward when she'd realized he'd been trying to make some damn point.

As if thinking about the man conjured him, Lucky's voice came from behind her. "Not feeling very sociable this morning, huh?"

Unnerved, JoJo whipped around so fast, she fell off the bale she was sitting on. A couple of stacked bales also toppled, bringing her to the floor of the loft in their midst. A heavy bale atop her, she glared up at Lucky, who found the situation amusing, if his choked laughter were any indication.

"The least you could do is help."

He stooped and started to lift the weight. "Something's stuck." He tried reaching a hand in between her body and the bale to investigate.

She smacked the searching fingers away before they caused trouble. "I'll do it, thank you." But her body tingled as if he'd actually touched her anyway.

"You asked for help." Lucky rocked back on his haunches and grinned at her. "I was only trying to be agreeable."

Sliding her hand down to her waist, JoJo found the problem. Her belt buckle was hung up on some bale wire. Fingers working frantically, she freed the metal piece.

"Got it."

And couldn't help herself. She rolled the bale off her...and onto Lucky, knocking him off his haunches.

"Hey!"

"Right. Hay!"

Snorting, JoJo tried to make a quick escape, but already freeing himself, Lucky shot out a hand, caught her by the ankle and dragged her back down next to him, her fall softened by loose hay that seemed to be everywhere now.

On the floor. In the air. In her clothes. Up her nose.

She sneezed and started to itch.

The itch transformed into something a bit more tormenting when Lucky slid over her, setting every nerve in JoJo's body afire.

"Don't mess with a Donatelli," he warned her. "We give as good as we get."

"Something in the genes?"

Even though his back was to the light, she couldn't miss the fleeting cheerless expression that passed over his features only to be replaced by the familiar devil-ish grin. *Uh-oh*. That meant he was up to something.

Squirming under him, JoJo said, "I think we'd better get back to the others."

"No hurry."

Pulse surging, she pushed at his chest. Futilely. She might as well try to move a wall.

"But they're probably wondering where we've dis-appeared to," she complained.

"They're not missing us," he promised.

Undoubtedly not. Still, she tried again. "I haven't seen much of the town."

"Not much to see."

Amazed that she was unable to think of a stronger excuse, she stared up at him mutely, wondering if he were feeling the same attraction she was or if he were tormenting her because he still thought she was re-porting to his father. No matter, she had no control over her own being. Her pulse began to pound faster, and her mouth went dry. Worse, there was this funny little catch in her breath that she only prayed he couldn't hear.

"Be truthful with yourself," Lucky whispered, making JoJo think he was going to probe again about her reasons for being there. But he surprised her when he said, "You want me as much as I want you."

"I...I..."

"Say it."

Unable to find her voice, JoJo wanted to deny it. She wouldn't admit to any such thing. Not about him. She trembled. Feared that he would kiss her again. She prepared to stop him. To stop herself.

Energy spent for naught.

A scraping outside the barn broke the fine thread that held them fast. Footsteps below told her they weren't alone.

"Anyone up there?"

"Adair!" JoJo cried, half in relief.

She would deal with the disappointment half later. This time, when she pushed at Lucky, he moved back and surged to his feet.

"We're up here," he announced, holding out his hand to JoJo.

She accepted his offer. His hand gripping hers was more stirring than she might have imagined. Heat sizzled up her arm. His look was equally hot before he let go. But she was nearly recovered by the time Adair's blond head popped over the edge of the loft.

At least she was recovered enough to say, "The view's pretty good from up here."

"Uh-huh."

JoJo realized Adair was staring at the imprints in the straw, at the bits clinging to them, and he was obviously filling in the blanks. JoJo beat fiercely at her clothing to rid herself of the evidence of her foolishness.

"Everyone had enough?" Lucky asked.

"I don't know. Have they?" Adair returned, tone amused as the men locked gazes for a moment.

Not liking the male-bonding thing going on here, JoJo muttered, "I have," and stomped to the ladder.

She practically slid down the thing in her hurry to put some distance between her and the situation that could so easily have gotten out of hand. How did this keep happening to her? How could she fall under the spell of a man who was arrogant, antagonistic and very probably dangerous.

Escaping the stable, she took a big, relieved breath to be out of his sphere of influence.

Across the street, Paula and Rocky were huddled together in the shelter of a building. They were conversing in low tones, looking pretty intent, until they noticed her. Paula didn't seem all that happy to be interrupted, but she put on one of her cheery smiles and waved JoJo over. Reluctantly, JoJo joined them, figuring the other woman must have been checking Rocky out.

"Lucky was saying something about getting back," JoJo told them.

"Okay by me," Rocky said.

Paula agreed. "I've had enough exploring for one day."

Seconds later, Lucky and Adair exited the stable. Both men seemed to be in good humor, JoJo noticed resentfully.

"Let's round 'em up!" Lucky said.

That Lucky paid her no more mind than the others smarted. Confused by his wavering attitude toward her, JoJo would be glad to head back to the ranch.

A few minutes later, they were on their way. Good timing, it seemed, for the sun was playing hide-and-seek with a couple of clouds rolling in over the area.

The male-bonding thing obviously still in progress, Lucky and Adair took the lead. Paula rode a comfortable distance behind them, with Rocky trying to keep up. Though Adair looked her way several times, seeming intent on hanging back to talk to JoJo, Lucky seemed equally determined to have his company. JoJo let the distance between her and the leaders grow. Eventually, Rocky dropped back, too, and rode with her. His bottom was thumping even more furiously against the saddle than it had on the way out. Some cowboy.

"So did Rimrock meet your expectations?" JoJo asked to be friendly.

"Sort of. I thought it'd be bigger, though."

"Towns out here were pretty small before the turn of the century. I read an article about some of them being only a handful of buildings—just the basics for prospectors to get supplies and such."

"I guess I've seen too many old Westerns."

"Movies do tend to glamorize things," she agreed.

Again, she thought it was strange that Rimrock had seemed as new to Adair as to the rest of them. Her gaze shifted ahead to the stuntman, still in the lead with Lucky. He was still glancing back at her every so often, as if he were keeping an eye on her. Maybe Adair hadn't been in the scenes shot at the old ghost town. If that had been the case, why hadn't he just said so?

JoJo crossed the dry wash, then suddenly realized Rocky wasn't beside her. She glanced over her shoulder. He'd fallen back even farther. He was six feet below, at the bottom of the arroyo and staring balefully at the climb up to the bank where she waited.

"You okay?"

"Yeah, just hungry."

And sore, though he obviously didn't want to admit it. "We'll be back at the ranch soon," she assured him. "Just lean forward so your weight's over Apache's neck. Then give him his head."

"I know that," Rocky insisted. "I was just giving him a breather."

Thinking the man had to keep his macho image, JoJo didn't say anything. She kept Spitfire in check, waiting for Apache to get up the side of the arroyo despite the bobbling weight of his rider. No doubt Rocky's sense of direction was as finely honed as his riding skills. If he got too far behind, he might get himself lost.

JoJo turned Spitfire and moved her out slowly enough so that the other horse could catch up.

They rode in silence for a while, before Rocky said, "You got straw in your hair."

She brushed the curls below her hat. "Did I get it all out?"

"Yeah, but there's more all down your back."

As flustered as if she'd been caught with Lucky, she grabbed the bottom of her vest and fluttered it, hoping to free the straw bits. Her hand brushed her backside, and she checked there, as well. Nothing.

She rode for a while before it hit her.

Nothing. Really nothing.

Her hand returned to her back pocket.

Flat!

"My wallet—it's gone!" And with a certainty, JoJo knew just where she'd lost it. Darn Lucky Donatelli anyway. "I've got to go back."

"To Rimrock?"

"I had my wallet when we got there. I don't care about the money, but my driver's license and credit cards..." Some kid had stolen her purse in New York once. Replacing everything had been a major pain, and one of her credit-card bills that kept bouncing from the old number to the new had been a nightmare that had taken months to get straightened out. "It must have dropped out of my pocket in the loft over the stable. Uh, that's where I picked up the hay. Tell the others where I am so no one thinks I got lost."

If *someone* would even care. Although she'd gotten plenty of attention from Adair, she hadn't noticed Lucky's looking back to see how she was doing, and they were three-quarters of the way back to the ranch. As a matter of fact, he and Adair were so far ahead now that they were small figures in the distance.

"I'll go with you," Rocky volunteered as she started to turn Spitfire.

She stopped the mare. "No need," she assured him, thinking about his tender bottom. The man would be sore enough without riding a couple of extra miles. "You go ahead and catch up with Paula. The sooner you get back, the sooner you eat," she said, giving him a graceful way out of the offer.

"You sure?"

"Go on. I can find my way back."

"Okay."

Glancing up at the sky, JoJo noted that more clouds had moved in. Rain was on its way. If she moved fast, however, she could probably get back to the ranch before the first splatter.

After making certain Rocky was all right—he was quickly catching up to Paula, boldly flapping his arms and legs to make Apache go faster—JoJo urged Spitfire into a canter, quickening the pace, yet keeping it easy enough so that she didn't wear out her mount.

Again they crossed the stone-lined arroyo, and this time JoJo realized the potential danger of a heavy rain. The now-dry basin would undoubtedly fill fast with rushing water that would be difficult and perhaps even unsafe to cross. She'd be back before that rain began, JoJo vowed, signaling Spitfire to get a move on.

When she came within sight of the town, she brought the mare back down to a walk to cool out, even though the wind was picking up and the sky was turning a truculent gray.

She dismounted in front of the jail, its hitching post closest to the stable.

Once inside, she headed straight for the ladder, re-playing in her mind every nuance of the wrestling match with Lucky, the event undoubtedly prompting her wallet to go astray. Even now, thinking about his body over hers left her a little light-headed. And she needed her full concentration, for this time, she had no light to guide her up to the hayloft. The sky had darkened ominously.

Forcing thoughts of Lucky to the back of her mind, she practically took two rungs at a time and, once on the upper level, crawled around on hands and knees, blindly digging through straw, raising enough hay dust to give her a sneezing fit. Settling on her haunches, waiting for the itching in her nose to subside, JoJo could hardly believe her ears when she heard the first drops of rain *pat-pat* against the stable's roof.

Frantic to get out of Rimrock before she was caught here for who knew how long, she ripped through the straw, holding her breath against inhaling more of the fine particles until finally her hand hit leather.

"Ta-da!"

Triumphantly, she retrieved the wallet even as lightning lit the loft. A roll of thunder followed, and after that came an instant deluge.

"Damn!"

The view out the window was of a solid wet curtain. Shoving the wallet into her back pocket, JoJo wondered what she was supposed to do now. She couldn't start out in the blinding rain—she'd never find her way back. She'd just have to sit it out and wait for a break in the weather. Then they could hightail it out of there.

Rain drove inside her shelter, and JoJo moved to shut the awkward moldering doors on their creaky hinges. The rain was so heavy she couldn't see down to the street.

Even so, that Spitfire was being drenched occurred to JoJo, and part of her thought to rescue and bring the poor horse into the dry stable. But then they would both be soaking wet, and what would that accomplish?

Besides, if they were back at the ranch, Spitfire would be pastured, with only a small lean-to acting as a puny half shelter against the rain for all the horses. Being wet wouldn't hurt the mare, so in the end, JoJo decided to stay put and make it up to Spitfire later with a nice rubdown and a few carrots or whatever else she could find for a treat.

Not having worn a watch, JoJo had no idea of how long she waited for the storm to diminish. A half hour? An hour? An eternity had passed before the sound of driving rain abated and the sky lightened marginally. She was able to see as much through the large crack between the hayloft doors since they no longer matched properly.

JoJo scrambled down the ladder and rushed through the stable and into the street. Mud sucked at her new leather boots as she hotfooted it toward the jail to retrieve Spitfire.

Suddenly she stopped, frozen, her heart lurching.

No horse.

JoJo tried to still the rising panic threatening to swallow her whole.

Chapter Seven

"Spitfire!" JoJo yelled.

Though she hoped the mare was within hearing distance, she received no answering whinny. Surely Spitfire wouldn't have wandered very far in that downpour. She spotted a piece of leather in the mud beneath the hitching post—the mare had pulled the reins free, no doubt to find shelter. JoJo ran, slid and slipped through the sandy muck to the back of the buildings, calling and whistling, but saw no flash of a chestnut hide.

No Spitfire.

Now what?

Frantic from quickly building stress, JoJo could hardly think clearly, yet it came to her that, without the mare, she had no choices. If she couldn't find Spitfire, she was going to have to walk back to the ranch house. Retracing her steps, she searched the ground for any prints not obliterated by the rain. Futile, she thought, until she realized the earth was kicked up in the street in a regular pattern, a messy trail leading out of town.

The mucked-up area was a bit broad to have been made by a single horse. Could there have been two of them, then? A lump the size of a melon grew in her throat as she thought of the implications. For a moment, she couldn't swallow.

Had someone with harmful intentions followed her back to Rimrock and purposely stolen her horse?

She wanted to believe this was simple misfortune, but instinct told her otherwise. Undoubtedly, this was no accident... not any more than the Bushwhacker incident had been. Nor any more than hearing what sounded like gunshots that first day out with Spitfire had been. Someone was doing more than trying to scare her away from the Macbride Ranch. Someone wanted her hurt.

She couldn't...wouldn't...think further than that.

Still, her mount's doing a disappearing act didn't make sense, for how could an unpleasant walk hurt her?

Perhaps not the walk... but someone waiting to ambush her along the way...

Heart beating to a weird rhythm, JoJo followed the mucky trail that eventually disappeared on the gravel road outside of town. Senses heightened by fear and fighting panic, she was aware of every sound, every movement, every nuance of her surroundings as she backtracked. She hurried, power-walking as best she could in the new boots, feeling the still-stiff leather rub through her socks against her heels and toes, knowing she would suffer later. She concentrated on what those feet were doing, putting one down before the other, finding a safe path, so she wouldn't have to think.

Wouldn't have to wonder if, even now, someone were watching, plotting against her.

Wouldn't have time to be paranoid.

Wouldn't go out of her mind.

JoJo recognized the welling panic, that same horrible sensation filling her as it had the day of the wedding when she'd thought she'd spotted Lester Perkins in the crowd. But chances were she *had* seen him, since he'd escaped from his psychiatric ward that very morning.

And he was still on the loose.

Not that Lester knew where she was, JoJo assured herself. He'd have no way of finding her.

Who, then, had been messing with her mind?

Don't mess with a Donatelli, Lucky had warned her in the hayloft. *We give as good as we get.*

He'd been teasing, though. She was certain of it. She didn't want to believe that Lucky could have spirited Spitfire away.

But someone in the seemingly friendly group must have, she thought. Unless . . .

Caroline hadn't come along, and JoJo was aware of what Lucky's sister thought of her. Caroline Donatelli probably knew the area like the back of her hand, since she'd been coming to the ranch for years. Could she have ridden out after the group, taking a slightly different route, just waiting for her chance to play a nasty trick on JoJo?

Renewed rain cut through JoJo's speculation. She was soaked in a minute, before she could even look around for shelter. Not that she knew of any. She didn't remember seeing a single overhang on her ride out.

No choice but to keep going.

Head down, she pressed through the torrent, her one motivating thought the safety of the ranch house, where she would have lots of company. Where she wouldn't be alone and afraid. That she probably had a two-hour walk ahead of her didn't daunt JoJo in and of itself. As a dancer, she was in great physical shape. Her body could take the exercise. And her boots even seemed to be cooperating—softening as they grew wetter, the leather molding around her feet.

But two hours was a long time to be an easy target.

Unable to see more than a few yards in any direction, she started jogging at an effortless pace. She couldn't keep this up all the way home, but she could alternate between jogging and walking, thereby cutting down the time that she would be isolated and vulnerable.

Cutting down the time she would be wet and cold.

Despite her quickened pace, JoJo was shivering. She rubbed her arms. Hugged herself closer. Concentrated so hard on thinking warm that she missed the drop in the ground until her feet met air.

Suddenly, JoJo went flying. She threw her arms out for balance and by good fortune managed to land right side up, one knee in soft, sucking sand. Quickly, she rose, then stood stock-still for a moment, legs shaking, her boot tips mere inches from surging water.

The arroyo.

Dear Lord, the very thing Lucky had warned them all about.

No longer a dry wash, the arroyo had become a miniriver, its current fast and treacherous. She could see bits of trees and other plants rushing by.

What now?

Not knowing any other route home, she would have to cut across here. She gazed up to the top of the bank and realized the wash had only half filled, maybe three feet or so. Waist-high water wasn't impossible to cross, even with a current. She could do it, JoJo thought. Though she couldn't see to the other side, she guessed the distance at barely a dozen yards. Of course she could do it.

She *had* to do it.

Spotting a tree limb swirling a short distance away, JoJo planted one foot in the ankle-deep water and reached. The limb was a bit too far out and sped past her fast. JoJo plunged a step farther, the water coming to her calf, and grabbed before the limb could get away. Quickly, she balanced the sturdy wood on end before the water could get her. The top came to her shoulder, exactly the right height for a staff.

Unwilling to wait any longer, for already the water was swelling, JoJo used the staff to check the wash's bottom several feet farther out. It seemed solid enough. Taking a big breath and offering up an even bigger prayer, she took a step forward. Not too bad. Here the water still swirled around her calves. Another few steps took her knee-deep.

Only twenty feet to go.

JoJo moved the staff, saw it plunge deeper this time. A thrill shooting through her stomach, she forced her legs to follow. Thigh deep now, she drove the staff forward, then her legs, repeating the movements until water swirled around her waist and the current buffeted her.

Not quite halfway, JoJo focused on the other bank, which she could barely see through the steady downpour. The next set of steps took her even deeper, however. Water rushed around her breasts, the current sucking, pulling at her. Her heart thundered, and she tried not to give in to panic.

Realizing she'd misjudged the depth, JoJo wrapped both hands around the tree limb and inched her way forward, at the same time working with the insistent current, allowing it to coax her downstream even as she drew closer to the other bank. Somehow, no matter how much progress she made, she was barely staying ahead of the rapidly rising water.

And in the distance, a roaring sound alerted her to added danger.

Exhaustion called for rest, but stopping even for a moment could be fatal. Instead, JoJo mustered her reserves and pushed her way several more yards toward shore. Her reward was waist-deep water. Adrenaline surging, she kept going, stumbling when she got to the far side of the wash.

Caught in the current, her staff sped off too quickly for her to react.

And the rushing sound loomed closer.

Fevered with the need to get away from the wash, JoJo pushed herself upright and began the rock-strewn climb that seemed much higher than she remembered. Or perhaps it was just the spot where she'd landed. But every time she took a step, she slid back. Rather than feet, she ascended in inches. Halfway up, she paused for just a moment, panting for her breath, listening to the rushing sound that was quickly becoming a roar. And she heard something else. A human voice.

"JoJo!"

The voice was faint—some distance away—but familiar. Lucky. She opened her mouth to answer, then froze. What if he was responsible for her being on foot? What if he'd come back to finish her off?

Clenching her jaw with determination, she started climbing again, ignoring the repeated echo of her name as his voice drew closer. Her hand found the top of the bank. Her fingers closed around what felt like stable rock. She levered her boot against the slippery soil and pushed upward only to see Lucky stalking her through the torrent, a dangerous, dark shape that fluttered and shifted.

"JoJo!"

"No-o-o!" she cried, frantically trying to gain the bank before he could reach her.

Once more her foot slipped on unstable earth, and everything happened in slow motion. Her body shooting out. Head turning toward the sound of a more imminent threat than Lucky. Eyes widening at the torrent of raging water loosed upon the arroyo as if a dam upstream had burst. Hanging on to the rock with a single hand, she felt as if her arm was about to separate from her shoulder.

Worse, her fingers burned . . . and began to slip.

Then a hand clamped around her wrist, and she looked up to see Lucky looming over her, yellow slicker flapping around him. "Get some footing if you can!" he yelled.

Too late. Water suddenly rushed around her dangling legs, threatening to swallow her whole. "I can't!"

Lucky threw himself backward onto the ground, his powerful maneuver thrusting her into the stone-encrusted bank and toward him. Breath knocked out of her at contact, JoJo still had the presence of mind to dig at the pebbled muck with a clawed hand, to fight the menacing water with kicking legs. Then suddenly she was free of nature's peril behind her, body shaking as she was drawn up against the all-too-human threat before her.

Even through the rain, JoJo could see Lucky's eyes. Stony accusation rather than the warmth she craved acknowledged her. Filled with conflicting emotions, JoJo wondered if she had just traded one perilous risk for another.

LUCKY HEAVED himself to his feet and JoJo with him. He'd wanted her gone, hadn't figured he'd care how. But letting her drown like a rat hadn't been part of his plan.

Grabbing hold of her arm, he dragged JoJo toward Silverado. She could hardly move. Only half stopping, he hoisted her up into his arms and kept going, his limp more pronounced by her weight. She was shaking. And though she didn't protest this time, she was trying to keep herself separate from him. She leaned away from his chest.

And Lucky was assaulted by a multitude of unwelcome and contradictory thoughts, first of which was that he wished she'd move closer, wrap her arms around his neck as if he wasn't some kind of damn pariah. Then again, hadn't he wanted her gone one way or the other?

He feared he now had the advantage.

A few yards from where he'd left his horse, he set her feet down, though he kept a steadying arm across her back.

"Think you can stand there while I mount?"

Mutely, she nodded her agreement, water pouring from her hat, which she'd managed to keep intact.

At least some part of her body was dry.

Picking up Silverado's reins that he'd left dangling on the ground so the gelding would stay put, Lucky swung up into the saddle. He held out his hand. JoJo stared at it. And then at him.

"Take it, or I'll leave you here!" he shouted above a clap of thunder.

Eyes bleak, she placed a hand that felt like ice in his. He removed his left foot from its stirrup so she could use it to mount. He swore he heard her boot squish as she hiked herself up. When she settled behind him, she fisted his rain slicker rather than get too close.

Irritated that she was acting as though he had the plague—and after he'd saved her life—Lucky ordered, "Get a grip, woman, or you'll fall off."

Obediently, she slid her arms around his middle and trembled against his back. From cold or fear? Maybe both. Conflicted as he seemed to be every time he was around her, Lucky cursed and signaled Silverado to move off. The ranch house was a good ride away, a half hour or better in this weather, so he sought a closer shelter.

Less than five minutes later, they were under a rocky overhang nestled within minor red sandstone formations. Lucky helped JoJo down, then dismounted himself. Retrieving a waterproof, battery-operated torch from where he'd tied it to his saddle roll, he drew both her and his horse toward an opening in the rock face.

"Where are you taking me?"

"Someplace dry."

"Why not the ranch?"

The fear and suspicion making her voice quaver should gratify him more than it did.

"Don't worry, I won't attack you," he said truthfully, unable to help adding, "You look like a drowned rat anyway."

"No thanks to you."

"It's my fault you were out in a storm?" Well, maybe not a rat. Her clothes were soaking wet, molding her body much too closely for a man's comfort. "I warned everyone this morning about how serious it could get." He stripped off the wet slicker and threw it over the saddle. "What happened to your horse anyway?"

"I thought *you* might have some ideas."

"I just bet you did," he groused.

A few more steps, and they were inside the cave that he and Nick and Caroline had discovered as kids. Flashing his torch beam around, Lucky noted the stack of firewood against the far wall. Someone had used the cave in recent years, as well. The remainder of a fire ring decorated the middle of the cave floor, and to one side, a crack in the ceiling dripped water. Though the fracture in the rock offered ventilation for a fire, Lucky knew it wasn't directly open to the sky.

He dropped Silverado's reins and shone the light on JoJo. "Get undressed."

Features indignant, she responded, "Get a life!"

Lucky sighed. "You want to chance pneumonia?"

"It'd be safer than chancing . . . other things."

He could sense her squirming inside. On the outside, she appeared every bit as defiant as usual.

"It's up to you. But there's a dry blanket wrapped in an oilcloth tied behind Silverado's saddle. I brought it because I figured you might need it."

"Oh."

Setting the torch on the cave floor, beam pointing away from the horse and woman and toward the stack of wood, Lucky busied himself building a fire. He kept his back to JoJo, but the sounds of her wet clothing plopping against the ground one item at a time echoed around him and burrowed inside his head.

As he rebuilt the fire ring—stones on the outside, larger pieces of wood in the center, kindling on top— Lucky imagined JoJo naked, wild red hair flaming around her shoulders, her long limbs pale and smooth, her breasts heavy and inviting. His reaction was not only spontaneous and completely natural, but demonstrated the tightness of his jeans in a particularly uncomfortable area. Before setting a match to the wood, Lucky guardedly adjusted.

A few minutes later, fire roaring, JoJo was seated as close to the flames as was prudent. Next to her, wet clothing was draped over equally wet boots, all drying before the fire. Wrapped in the blanket, she dabbed one corner of the material at the straggles of wet hair trailing her shoulders. She was also wiggling around, an indication the wool was scratchy.

Lucky stripped off his chambray shirt and threw it at her. "This might be a bit more comfortable."

"Thanks."

At least she no longer sounded as if she thought he was going to offer her up as coyote bait.

Lucky removed Silverado's saddle. Fortunately, he'd padded the old horse's back with double saddle blankets as usual and so was able to use one to wipe down the wet animal. By the time he was finished, JoJo was wearing his shirt and sitting cross-legged before the fire, one edge of the blanket drawn over her bare feet and legs. She'd left plenty of room.

For him to sit next to her?

Knowing trouble was thumbing its nose at him, he accepted her unspoken invitation. "Don't mind if I do."

Feeling a little too exposed wearing only Lucky's shirt, JoJo was thankful he left a bit of room between them. "I suppose I should thank you for coming to my rescue."

Even though he'd been conveniently at hand when she'd needed rescuing, JoJo reminded herself. Again.

"Now don't go feeling obligated on me or anything."

His sarcasm not lost on her, she said, "I don't. I mean . . . thank you . . . really."

He was staring at her in the same way he had when he'd pulled her out of the drink. As if he were angry or . . . resentful? Confused, guarded, JoJo shifted her weight, pulled her knees to her chest and wrapped her arms around her legs. Not that she was cold anymore.

The fire crackled and she stared into its depths as if she could read its heart. "What made you come after me?" As if she could read *his* heart.

He pulled off a wet boot. "Vincent was busy."

The answer made her throat tighten. "I mean, what made you think it was necessary?"

"I didn't realize how far behind everyone was until it started to rain." Lucky removed the other boot. "I was raiding the fridge. Then Paula and Rocky dragged in, and he said you'd gone back to Rimrock for your wallet. Damn fool thing for you to do!"

Temper flaring, JoJo asked, "Have you ever lost your wallet? Do you know what a pain in the rear it is to replace all your ID and credit cards?"

Again, he gave her the angry face as he threw down the boots near the fire. "Do you know what a pain in the rear it would've been if I'd shown up just a minute or so later?"

JoJo knew. She might not have made it. Still, she argued, "I would have been just fine if I weren't on foot."

"Whose fault is that? And don't say mine," he warned her.

Remembering she'd practically accused him of knowing what happened to Spitfire, and right after he'd dragged her out of the wash, she shifted guiltily.

"At first, I thought maybe Spitfire pulled loose while I was waiting out the storm in the stable...but that's about as likely as Bushwhacker's listening to music from the Caribbean because he wanted to dance," she admitted. Her laugh was shaky. "I'm beginning to realize that someone around here doesn't like me much."

"Apparently. You wouldn't have any guesses?"

"Other than you?" She returned his glare. It was the truth. He'd wanted her out from the get-go. "Try Sister Caroline of the Rotten Attitude."

He started at the nickname, but she swore he swallowed a smile, as well.

"Caroline can be unpleasant when she feels threatened," Lucky admitted, "but she's all talk. She'd never physically hurt anyone."

"You don't know that."

"I know my sister."

"Really? When you haven't seen her in...how many years were you gone?"

"Six. But leopards don't change their spots."

"She's definitely got some questionable spots," JoJo argued from personal experience.

"Caroline defends what she sees as hers. She's got a mouth on her...as do other women I've met recently," he stated flatly, expression saying he meant *her*. He stretched his damp feet toward the flames. "But she knows where to draw the line."

Personally, JoJo couldn't help but wonder if Lucky weren't fooling himself. She didn't want to argue about Caroline, though. She didn't have the energy.

"I hope you're right" was all she said.

"Who else around here doesn't like you?"

"I don't know."

"Take a guess."

"I haven't done anything to anyone!" she insisted. "You're the only one who thinks I have!"

An awkward silence filled the small cave, threatening to smother her. Too aware of the man on the other side of the blanket, JoJo concentrated on her clothes, willed them to dry so she could get properly dressed. Protection. That's what she needed. Being half-naked and too close to Lucky for comfort, she almost wished he hadn't found her. Almost. She wasn't ready to pack it in yet, and who knew if she could have survived the flash flood without him.

"I really did come to the ranch for a rest," JoJo assured Lucky. "I swear I'm not in on some plot with your father. What is it with you and him anyway?"

He gave her a searing look, then surprised her when he said, "You have no idea of what it's like to have Sally Donatelli as a father."

"So tell me."

"Before or after he was incarcerated?"

"Whenever."

JoJo could see that Lucky was tight with remembering, his body filled with tension. The newly healed scar on his forehead throbbed, seeming to take on a life of its own. She wondered if he really wanted to talk about anything so personal. If he could make himself do it.

"Hey, I'm an objective observer here, okay?" she said. "I know you both. I'd like to have some idea of what I'm dealing with. Is that too much to ask?"

Lucky's tension intensified as he began, "Sally managed to keep us away from the business." He used his father's first name as if he were detached from the story. "He kept us fooled, thinking we were a big, happy family. He always said there wasn't anything he wouldn't do for us. And then he was arrested and tried and locked away, and we realized he'd betrayed us all. Mama loved him so much, being away from him broke her heart. She died a couple of years later."

"And you hold your father responsible."

"Damn straight!"

More than twenty years after the fact, grief was obviously still ripping Lucky up inside. And JoJo was astonished that he'd allow himself to reveal something so incredibly intimate.

Something that made him human.

Vulnerable.

Till now, he'd kept his emotional space, probably the reason the sparks between them confused her so. She hadn't been able to justify her being attracted to a man who was so hostile...who was so closed off that he couldn't take anything at face value...who couldn't believe her when she told him she wasn't working for his father.

How could she have known he was hurting and why?

Her own father had died when she was a kid, but she still remembered how much her mother had suffered. She expected that if there was any caring between two people and one died, the survivor would have a difficult time. Especially a survivor who'd gone to great pains to create a "big, happy family" as Sally had.

"You don't believe your father loved your mother?" she asked.

"How could a man like that love anyone?"

Thinking two decades of repressed anger were talking, she asked, "You don't believe Sally mourned your mother every bit as much as you did?"

But Lucky skirted the question. "If he hadn't gone to prison—"

"She might have died anyway."

JoJo didn't know the cause of his mother's death, yet she was fairly certain a person couldn't really die of a broken heart. But Lucky had been the youngest of the siblings. He'd been just a kid, and had obviously drawn conclusions straight from his own immature, too-tender heart. Conclusions that he'd lived with all these years.

"When my mother was sick, Sally had his lawyer draw up some papers making Vito Tolentino our legal guardian if anything happened to her. Vito took care of us like we were his own kids."

JoJo already knew Vito Tolentino, Sally's right-hand man and Nick's best man. "Your father made sure you were all right, even from prison."

"We weren't all right. Nick got into trouble running a floating craps game in back of the high school."

"But Nick told me Vito took care of that problem, knocked some sense into him, made sure Nick studied hard enough to get into Harvard."

"What about Caroline? She took over for Mama when she was way too young. She became obsessed with Nick and me because she was afraid she'd lose us like she did our parents. She's never made a life for herself. Never trusted any man enough to fall in love."

It made JoJo feel some compassion for Lucky's sister. And for Lucky, who didn't trust anyone, either.

"I'm not saying the way Sally made a living was okay," she said. "But he did pay for his crimes with eighteen years of his life."

"Of all our lives. Nick's and Caroline's and mine." Lucky's laugh was bitter. "And he went straight from a jail cell back to his business."

"A different business than before," she reminded him. "Nick saw to that."

"Nick was walking a tightrope those years he was in charge. He was trying to change things without making more enemies. That takes careful planning. And lots of time." Lucky's visage was grim when he added, "He didn't have enough time to finish what he started."

"And you think your father went back to the old ways?"

"Like I said before, a leopard doesn't change its spots."

JoJo couldn't argue with him. Actually, Lucky was probably right about Sally to some degree. His father enjoyed power. Control. Nick suspected Sally's hanging on to a few old interests was a ploy to get him back running the family business. What better lure than to shake up Nick with the thought that—if he didn't finish what he'd started—his father might do more prison time?

Convoluted thinking, perhaps, but then Sally was a complex and crafty man.

Thank goodness Nick was too savvy to buy into the scheme. Caroline was a different story, though, JoJo knew. She'd take over for her father in a New York minute. All he'd have to do would be to give her the nod.

And Lucky was still something of an enigma to her. He had strength, will, a fierceness that inspired just the proper amount of fear—all traits that Sally possessed. He'd be furious if she pointed out the similarities between him and his father, however. He plainly wanted nothing to do with Sally, had disappeared rather than meet the old man head to head.

That she was starting to understand Lucky a little frightened her, but JoJo couldn't help herself from pressing him some more.

"By cutting out your father, you've managed to put fact to Caroline's fears." JoJo didn't miss the flash of guilt across Lucky's features. "And how do you think Nick feels? And Vito, the man who raised you? I know he loves Nick and would do anything for him, and I'd bet he feels the same about you."

"They understand."

"All except Caroline."

"She's forgiven me."

Perhaps. JoJo thought about family, how difficult it was for her to be separated from her mother and brother sometimes, even though they kept in contact by letter and phone. How much she wished she had her father. She couldn't believe Lucky was unaffected by what was his own doing.

"You'll have to stop running someday, you know."

Features placid, he stated, "I'm not running anywhere."

"You are. What are you afraid of, Lucky?"

His features tightened. "Nothing."

"That you might still have feelings for the man you blame for your mother's death?"

An outright glare was her answer.

"Or that he might suck you back into the business?"

"Never!"

"Then what?"

A short silence was followed by his quiet certainty. "I'm afraid I might kill him."

The way he said it sent a shudder coursing down her spine. For a moment, JoJo fully believed that Lucky Donatelli was capable of murder. For a moment, she was truly afraid of him. Then she remembered he'd just saved her life and felt like an ingrate. As he'd said about Caroline, talking and doing weren't the same thing.

Responding to his pain, she inched closer and placed a hand on his arm. "You're not just angry at your father. You're angry at yourself."

"You don't know what you're talking about," he returned, jaw hard, arm tightening under the pads of her fingers.

"I think I do. I fell in love with a man who was using me. I was ready to marry a murderer." She could see it now like a movie playing in her head. How had she not recognized the villain in her own life? "For all I know, he might have murdered me, too."

And maybe someone was trying to murder her now, she thought despondently, feeling so out of the loop that she couldn't figure out why or who.

Slowly, Lucky faced her. Their gazes locked, he asked, "And you're angry at yourself?" He sounded amazed.

She nodded. "For being stupid. Shortsighted. Gullible. Aren't those familiar feelings?" He didn't have to answer. She could see she'd hit a nerve. "The difference between our situations is that Marco never loved me. Sally loves you more than you can probably believe right now. But maybe eventually you'll understand that sometimes what a person does, doesn't dictate who that person loves."

He digested that for a moment, then asked, "Are you up to forgiving Marco?"

"No." She had no doubts. Any soft feelings she'd had for the man were vanquished. "But he used me to gain his vengeance. His actions were *against* me."

"And what you're saying is that my father acted *despite* us?"

"There *is* a difference."

JoJo could tell Lucky was considering the fine points of her argument. But if he was swayed, he didn't admit to it. She knew one thing, though. He loved his father. If he didn't, he wouldn't still be carrying around all that anger and resentment from his childhood. If he didn't, he wouldn't have disappeared just before Sally Donatelli was released from prison so that he didn't have to face him.

"Are you real?" Lucky suddenly asked, looking at her as if he were truly seeing her for the first time.

JoJo's mouth went dry, and she had trouble taking an even breath, as if the moment of truth had come . . . with her not knowing how to respond.

Chapter Eight

Staring at Lucky's well-formed biceps below the ragged edges of the sleeveless white T-shirt, JoJo joked, "Flesh and blood." *And all woman,* she feared, if the light-headedness she was suddenly experiencing were any indication. "Here, pinch me."

Not expecting him to take her up on it, she held out her arm. His loose shirtsleeve slid halfway to her elbow, the soft cotton whisking along her skin like the lightest, most sensual touch. Her imagination stirred, perhaps because she knew the cloth had touched him before her, and her skin pebbled with an erotic chill. Then Lucky wrapped his fingers around her wrist, gently imprisoning her, sharing his heat with her. As she recognized the imprint of each finger on her flesh, he pulled her closer.

"Either you're real," he said softly, slipping his thumb pad along her sensitive palm until she had to stifle a gasp, "or I'm the biggest fool around."

Heart thumping, she whispered, "Not the *biggest* fool."

She reserved that distinction for herself. After what Marco had pulled on her, she should keep her distance from this man. And she only wanted to get closer. Both were sons of crime bosses. Both had been warped emotionally by their fathers in ways she could only try to understand. No matter how open Lucky had been for a few minutes, she knew as little about him as she had Marco.

Part of her was definitely afraid.

But part of her was willing to be tempted, not just by the physical attraction that sizzled between them alone, but additionally by the part of Lucky that she figured few people knew about. He'd gotten to her on a level that went beyond basic instinct.

He'd touched her heart.

No wonder she couldn't move when he leaned closer, his mouth softly catching hers. She was hardly breathing when he drew back a few inches, one side of his face dark, the other licked by the red glow of the fire.

She touched his jaw, his cheekbone, his brow. Just as she'd been wanting to do for days. Her fingers explored the scar that would soon fade. With each new touch, his breathing grew more audible. She smiled. The half-light softened his features, made them welcoming rather than harsh. After what she'd been through earlier, she needed *welcoming*. She needed more.

Assurance. Comfort.

His touch. His mouth on hers.

She thought she might go out of her mind if he didn't kiss her again.

"What are we doing?" she asked through a growing haze of longing.

"Anything you want."

When she sighed in answer, he slid a hand along her jawline and behind her ear, his fingers splaying across the back of her neck, then cradling her head before he kissed her, this time more deeply. She didn't resist his using the leverage to bring her with him when he reclined on the blanket. Didn't resist when he hooked a hand at the small of her back and pressed until she edged over, landing softly and half on top of him. One of her knees fell between his, and the pulsing hardness along her thigh told her what he wanted of her.

Truthful with herself, JoJo admitted she wanted Lucky, too. They'd been leading up to this intimate confrontation since the first night, when he'd caught her in the hallway. For days now, they'd been playing a mating dance. Taunting each other. Sizing up one another. Trying to deny the inevitable, each for his or her own reason.

But JoJo didn't deny Lucky when he slipped a hand beneath the chambray shirt and ran it slowly over her naked buttocks and up along her spine. She held her breath as he explored her waist, then the fullness of her breast. Their mutual sounds of satisfaction filled the primitive cave, competed with the sudden crackle of a spitting log.

His kiss deepened, tongue probing, as the rough pads of his fingers ventured along the inside swell of her breast. Her nipples tightened even before he claimed one. He thumbed, circled, tugged at the sensitive flesh, until she began moving restlessly, her hips tilting, her thighs spreading around his jean-clad leg.

"Wait!" she gasped softly, pulling away long enough to unbuckle his belt, her fingers tracing the engraved bull and rider.

Lucky watched her through slitted eyes, seemingly content to let her do what she would with him for the moment. Self-conscious, JoJo was glad she was wearing his shirt, and yet she felt more sensual, more alluring than if she were completely undressed. She unzipped his jeans, peeled them and his briefs from his waist. He raised his hips. She pulled the garments farther. Then he was kicking them off, drawing her forward, spreading her thighs around his hips.

His hand slid under the shirt, finding her woman's center. His fingers glided easily over the slick flesh, the folds already opened for his touch. Eyes fluttering, she let her head hang back and breathed slow and deep, her inner rhythm set by his fingers.

But inevitably, JoJo wanted more. Pressure building inside, she leaned forward, her hand smoothing the flesh of his thigh, tracing a small surgical scar over his hip. Undoubtedly, new surgery, the reason he limped at times. Then she forgot about unpleasant things. She found and stroked him. Lucky gasped, stilled for a moment, then wrapped both hands around her hips and drew her up and over him.

She slid home with a sigh.

And with a groan, Lucky clutched her to him as if he'd never let go, then rolled, landing her on her back beneath him. A happy laugh escaped JoJo as he lay quietly on top of her, his mouth exploring from her breast to her shoulder to the tender spot beneath her ear. Somewhere along the way, the laugh caught in her throat as the sensuality of his actions seized her. With each new contact, JoJo flowered inside, opening up to Lucky, taking him deeper.

Breathing as choppily as if he'd run a fast mile, he nuzzled his face in her hair. "I didn't expect this," he whispered, his teeth tugging at her ear. "I didn't expect that I'd let you get to me like this."

For an instant, JoJo's heart skipped a beat as his words registered. She wasn't certain how to take them. It sounded as if he still thought her an emissary of his father.

But it was too late for doubts to prevent the inevitable, for as Lucky began to move inside her, JoJo's body overrode her mind. She couldn't stop him. Couldn't stop herself. Her need was stronger than her misgivings. Passion caught her in a tight embrace and wouldn't relent.

She rocked her hips, arched her back, rode her legs up along his. She fairly sang with the pleasure that increased and multiplied until she could stand it no more. She dug her nails into his shoulders, his name a throaty moan on her lips. And as if that simple cry were the greatest aphrodisiac, Lucky buried his answer in her hair as his body began to shudder.

JoJo shuddered with him, her fall from the zenith perhaps quicker than his, the memory of his whispered words once again intruding.

BY THE TIME the rain let up and they were on their way back to the ranch, JoJo had convinced herself that she'd been too sensitive about Lucky's impassioned declaration during their lovemaking. He'd merely been expressing his amazement that he wanted her after all the emotional warfare between them. She was feeling the same surprise.

Surprise and doubt.

Rather than dwell on whether or not she'd made a mistake by landing in Lucky's arms, however, JoJo chose to think of their tryst as inevitable, though not necessarily an indication of what the future might hold for them. Undoubtedly, she'd be heading back to Las

Vegas in a matter of days, while Lucky probably never wanted to set foot in that town again. Who knew where he would be in a month. Back on the rodeo circuit? Or maybe on some oil rig in Texas.

Behind Lucky on Silverado, JoJo laid her cheek against his back. She didn't want to think about the situation too closely. If she'd thought about it to begin with, she might have kept her distance. The circumstances had caused her to lose her head. Coming so close to death had instigated her following her instincts rather than her logic.

And from the way Lucky kept his own counsel on the ride back to the ranch, JoJo suspected he was having the same doubts.

And so she was relieved when they arrived, stopping near the pasture. Lucky helped her down, then dismounted himself, dropping Silverado's reins on the ground despite the muck. The Appaloosa stood stock-still as he had in the rain.

Vincent appeared from a nearby outbuilding, a large shed that held the saddles and bridles. "Figured you'd be along any time, now that the weather broke."

Lucky pushed his hat back. "Have you seen the mare?"

"She pranced in here 'bout a quarter of an hour ago," the wrangler said, giving JoJo a sideways look.

"Spitfire's all right?" she asked.

"Right as rain." Vincent guffawed at his own joke. "She's in the pasture with the others. I was just checking over her tack—she tore her reins up to get free."

JoJo started. "She ripped through the leather?"

"She's some strong little mare."

Could it be? Had Spitfire gotten loose by herself rather than by another human hand?

"Where'd you leave the reins?" Lucky asked.

Vincent leaned through the doorway of the shed and pointed. "Right there."

"Take care of my horse, would you?"

Without a word to her, Lucky disappeared inside, and Vincent loosened the cinches on Silverado's saddle. Standing in the doorway, while Lucky took a careful look at the leather reins, JoJo remembered the bit of leather she'd spotted under the hitching post in Rimrock. She also felt a little weird. Lucky hadn't said anything of significance to her since leaving the cave.

The same applied when he left the shed a moment later and he seemed too preoccupied to even notice her.

"Well?" she demanded, forcing his attention her way. "What did you see?"

All he said was "Old leather ripped up good."

"Told ya," Vincent said as he lugged the saddle into the shed.

Lucky headed for the house. JoJo tracked after him, resentment growing. She practically had to jog to keep up with his long-legged stride.

Why couldn't he say something, anything, to put her at ease?

"We thought you'd both drowned," Caroline said the moment they walked through the front door.

JoJo couldn't help herself. "Disappointed?"

She stared at the other woman, watching for just a flicker of guilt, but unfortunately, she spotted no particular emotion to arouse suspicion. Maybe no guilt was to be had—not from anyone. Maybe she'd imagined the muddy tracks had been made by two horses rather than one.

"I was about to round up a posse and go after the two of you myself," Eli pronounced.

Other than Vincent, all the current residents of the ranch were present—Adair, Paula, Rocky and Flora in addition to Caroline and Eli. Every one of them seemed truly concerned and glad to see her unharmed, JoJo realized, but she couldn't help but suspect one of them was a poker-faced liar.

"What happened?" Paula asked JoJo breathlessly.

Lucky beat JoJo to it. "Spitfire pulled free from the hitching post back in Rimrock. JoJo had to walk back. She was crossing the wash when I found her."

JoJo wondered why he gave them such a carefully edited version of what had really happened...why he'd minimized the danger she'd been in.

Expression peculiar, Adair said, "You were gone an awful long time."

"We took shelter in a cave," JoJo said. "Lucky built a fire. That's where we dried off."

She was relieved that Lucky didn't elaborate on this part of the story.

"I had a feeling I should've gone with you," Rocky muttered. "None of this would ever have happened."

"I guess I should have listened to you," JoJo said agreeably.

Even though she knew that Rocky would have held her up, that they would have gotten caught in the downpour before getting back to Rimrock. But at least she would have made it back on her own horse rather than parked behind Lucky.

He'd already given her reason to have mixed feelings on that score.

"As it was," Paula told her, "Rocky and I were caught in the downpour. Lucky and Adair rode so far ahead, they just disappeared from view. We got lost, so we circled around in the rain for a while, trying to find our way home." She sighed. "Not that I minded, really. It was an adventure. Not as exciting as yours, of course, but we did have a few mishaps of our own."

"I made a big pot of chili for lunch," Flora told JoJo before Paula could elaborate further. "Perhaps you would like some to warm you inside."

"I'm warm enough, but thanks," JoJo told the housekeeper. "Maybe I'll have some later for dinner." Though her stomach was feeling a little hollow now, she didn't think she could choke the food down. Not until she had some time to breathe without so many sets of eyes on her. "I can heat it up myself when I'm ready to eat."

"Then if you don't need me, I will go," Flora announced.

"Sure. It's fine with me."

The housekeeper nodded and made for the back door.

"We were thinking about going into Sedona for dinner," Paula said with her usual enthusiasm. Her long nails threaded through her hair and hooked it behind her ear. "There are a couple of really neat places in town. We thought we'd go Mexican tonight. Giant margaritas and all. Don't worry, we'll wait for you to get cleaned up and everything—"

JoJo cut her off. "I'd rather just hang out here."

"I'll stay, too," Adair volunteered.

Uncomfortable with his seeming concern, JoJo forced a smile. "Go, please. No problem."

"I don't consider keeping you company a problem."

Tensely, she insisted, "I could use a little time alone."

As Adair looked from her to Lucky, his eyebrows raised. "Uh-huh."

"Don't patronize me!" JoJo said, voice rising. "Just go!" Heat rose along her neck.

Paula shot to her feet and announced, "I'm absolutely starving. If you guys don't get me into town and fast, I'm going to swoon from hunger."

"That trip to the past affected your speech," Adair said, laughing. "Swoon?"

"Let's go," Caroline agreed, moving closer to the blond man. She glanced over at Lucky. "Surely *you'll* come."

"I'll take a pass this time. Eli and I have some work to do."

"Tonight?"

"I've been gone all day."

"I'm sure it could wait till tomorrow," Caroline insisted.

"I suppose . . . if I wanted it to."

Caroline gave Lucky a sour expression that she turned on JoJo before leaving in Adair's reluctant wake. But if his sister had any ideas that Lucky wanted to be alone with *her,* JoJo thought, Caroline was sadly mistaken.

Lucky seemed restless, itchy. He rambled around the room, refusing to look directly at her.

Hurt, JoJo crossed her arms and glared at him, willing him to recognize her presence.

Eli broke the uncomfortable silence. "I take it you wanna go over to the Wrangler's Roost."

"You take it right." Lucky was already turning toward the left wing and his bedroom. "Just give me a few minutes to clean up."

"Will do." Then Eli looked at her. "Uh, I can wait for Lucky over at the Roost."

"No, don't leave."

"I thought you wanted to be alone."

"I wasn't feeling festive enough for an evening out." JoJo sank onto a couch, relishing its comfort. She was exhausted, both physically and emotionally. "That doesn't mean I couldn't use someone to talk to for a few minutes."

"That Adair fella volunteered . . . but I expect you have a hankering to talk about Lucky." He grinned at her. "So what do you wanna know?"

She wanted to know everything. Every detail of the way Lucky lived. How he thought. What his dreams were. Even what he planned to do next would be a start. Obviously, he'd come to some kind of crisis about his own identity, or he wouldn't have stepped foot on the Macbride Ranch, where his father might get word of him.

Or maybe that was the point. Maybe Lucky was ready for a showdown with the old man, even if he couldn't admit it.

Not knowing if Lucky had ever shared his past with Eli, she chose to begin with something totally innocuous. "How long ago did the two of you hook up?"

"Coming on five years."

"You met where? At a rodeo?"

"Shucks, no. We only been doin' the rodeo circuit for the past coupla years." Eli chuckled and shook his head. "Actually, we met in jail in a town in east Texas."

"Jail?" Not expecting that, JoJo started. "What for?"

With a straight face, Eli told her, "I had this unfortunate misunderstanding with a grouchy cashier at a local café over some money."

Pulse racing, she asked, "What about Lucky?"

"*Whew-ee.* You ask the tough ones."

"Do you answer them?"

Eli sucked in his cheeks, then, expression downright serious, said, "Lucky tried his best to kill a man with his bare hands." A chill shot down JoJo's spine.

I'm afraid I might kill him, Lucky had said of his own father.

JoJo guessed she'd been right to fear that Lucky Donatelli might be violent. Anger always seemed to simmer just below his surface. But before she could dig for the details of the incident that had landed him in jail, JoJo heard a door open. She glanced down the hall to see Lucky, dressed in a fresh shirt and a scowl, advancing on them.

"What are you two plotting?"

Eli's features went blank. "Just passin' time, my friend. Just passin' time."

"Then let's get out of here." Finally, at the door, he spoke directly to JoJo. "A hot shower and that chili would do you a world of good."

As if he cared, she thought resentfully, noting how flat and devoid of emotion his gray eyes were. "A lot of things would do me some good."

Like a hug and a reassurance that she hadn't made a fool of herself with him. But no hug or reassurance was forthcoming. Not even a soft look that would have warmed her insides. Lucky was gone in a flash, Eli with him.

Leaving JoJo wondering if Lucky hadn't in some way tried to punish his father by bedding her without falling into what he thought of as a trap.

That and his almost killing a man raised her suspicions about him all over again.

"WHAT IN TARNATION'S going on?" Eli asked the moment he and Lucky stepped into the Wrangler's Roost.

Figuring his friend meant between him and JoJo, Lucky wasn't about to be open on that issue, not when he didn't know the answer himself. After their getting as close as two people could, if only for a short while, his feelings toward the redhead were more mixed than ever. Half of him wanted her gone, so that he wouldn't be reminded of his father every time he looked at her. So that he wouldn't wonder if she'd played him for the sucker, after all.

The other half wanted to abscond with her, ride off into the night with her on Silverado and leave his past far behind. Make a fresh start.

But this was no Western movie. This was his life. And he had a real future to think of.

"Why don't we go over the plans again?" he said to Eli.

"Not until I get some answers."

Lucky glared. "You were never this interested in one of my women before."

Not that he'd had any women in exactly the same way in the past. Rather, he'd had temporary companions, who'd hitched along for the ride until one of them got tired of being together—most of the time him. Lucky was certain that wasn't JoJo's style. And he feared that he'd started something that couldn't be stopped.

"None of your women ever had so much bad luck in such a short time before," Eli clarified. "Yesterday it was Bushwhacker, now this missing-horse business. It *is* just bad luck, right?"

"Could be."

When he didn't elaborate, Eli set himself down in a leather chair and stretched out. "I got all the time in the world."

Eli could be a stubborn son of a mule, so Lucky admitted, "Her horse came back. Vincent said the reins were torn up—that the mare was strong enough to pull free."

"And you didn't believe it."

"I checked the reins over myself," Lucky admitted. "The leather was ragged. Mostly. But the edges looked different. Smoother."

"Like someone took a knife to 'em?"

"Like that," Lucky agreed.

"You tell the woman?"

He shook his head. He should have, no doubt. But he'd had too much going around in his mind to think clearly. Including JoJo. What to think about what had happened between them. What to do about her now.

"Probably for the best," Eli said.

Startling Lucky. "Why?"

"You tell her too much, you'll spook her good."

"Too late to stop that from happening," he said, remembering how scared JoJo had been. Her fright had driven her into his arms, he was certain.

"Then why hasn't she packed her bags and skedaddled?"

Was Eli just asking or did he sound disappointed? Lucky stared at the man he called a friend. Surely Eli couldn't have taken his earlier complaints about JoJo to heart. . . .

"You wouldn't know anything about those reins being cut, would you?"

"Lucky, you and me are like this," Eli said, holding two fingers together. "We each know how the other thinks."

Right. Once a con man, always a con man. Lucky knew Eli would never get grifting completely out of his system. But that didn't make him dangerous.

"Then you didn't try to get rid of JoJo because you knew I wanted her gone?"

Eli barked a laugh. "If I thought you needed help handling a woman, I'd find myself another partner."

Lucky laughed, too, and felt the tension start to drain out of him.

Until he realized that Eli hadn't said no.

A HOT SHOWER, a bowl of chili and she was ready to rock 'n' roll.

JoJo stood staring at the bedroom doors in the wing opposite hers and made her choice—Rocky Franzone's room first. The current residents had barely been gone for thirty minutes. She had at least an hour, more likely two. She planned on putting the time to good use, though she had no clue as to what to look for. She was working blind.

Thankful the doors locked only from the inside, she entered Rocky's bedroom and flipped on the light.

She'd already faced the fact that someone had been trying to create an unfortunate accident for her. Other than Caroline, all the other people staying at the ranch were strangers. Including Lucky. And while she wasn't about to discount Caroline, she didn't want to over-look any possible suspects—she had reason to doubt just about everyone but Flora and Eli.

The room was neat, the drawers empty but for some underwear and socks. A single suitcase—a big duffel, really—sat at the bottom of the closet beneath a pair of jeans and a clean shirt. Nothing suspicious but the lack of clothes. Rocky was traveling light when he'd talked about being in the area to get a job.

Actually, Rocky had talked about hooking up with a friend to get a job *wrangling* when he couldn't even sit a horse properly. By contrast, Paula rode as if she'd had years of professional—and expensive—training. She definitely was capable of having ridden to Rim-rock and back to the ranch pretty quickly. As was Adair, who'd been evasive about being part of the *Call of the West* movie shoot in the ghost town.

JoJo entered Paula Gibson's room next. The other woman had brought enough clothes for a month. She checked the labels on some of the fancier garments and recognized a couple of the names. Just as she'd suspected. Designer clothes on a secretary's salary? Not highly likely. Still, Paula had been married until recently, and her husband could have been well enough off to afford Paula's expensive tastes.

Before leaving the room, JoJo checked a magazine on the nightstand that stood open to an advertise-ment about a summer horse auction in Virginia. She flipped to the cover. *Hunter Jumper.* The issue was from the previous month...and had been mailed to P. Carbury at a Miller Valley, Maryland, address. Ei-ther a friend had sent Paula the issue, or some tourist had left it where Paula had spotted and confiscated it.

All the magazine did was confirm the woman's interest in English riding.

Refusing to be discouraged, JoJo proceeded to Adair Keating's room. His clothes were of good quality and a quantity between that of Rocky and Paula. What she hoped to find in his dresser drawers was some sign that he was a stuntman—either résumés or glossy photos that would confirm he'd been working on a movie as stated.

But from beneath his silk underwear, JoJo pulled an item that made her heart trip a beat. Her skin crawled at she stared at the hated object.

Why did Adair have a gun?

Chapter Nine

JoJo's mind roiled with the discovery of the lethal-looking handgun. If those noises that startled Spitfire that initial day *had* been gunshots, this might be the firing weapon. Adair had been the first of the paying guests to arrive at the ranch, she realized. As a matter of fact, he'd been in the house when she'd come back from that ride.

Could he have set off those shots, then taken up residence to lie in wait for her?

If so... why?

She recounted the Bushwhacker incident. While Paula and Rocky had gone off together, Adair had sprawled on the couch as if he'd intended on taking a nap. But had he? Or had he taken the opportunity to lock her inside an enclosure with a dangerous bull?

JoJo wrestled between returning the handgun to its drawer and confiscating it. If Adair noticed the weapon was gone... She didn't want to give him the advantage of knowing she was on to him, just in case he was the guilty one.

How to tell if the weapon had been fired recently?

She quickly figured out how to pull the magazine from the handle, then experienced a letdown when she found all of the bullets nestled snugly in place. Of course, Adair could have finished off one round, then replaced the clip.

On impulse, she emptied the magazine, popping one bullet at a time and stuffing them into her pants pockets. At least she could render the weapon temporarily useless. Just in case. Feeling better—a bit safer—she replaced the handgun, careful to hide it under the silk underwear exactly as she'd found it.

Now, what to do about Adair? How could she figure out whether or not he was the one to have instigated those accidents? And why? What motive could he possibly have for wanting her hurt or worse?

From the moment he'd arrived, Adair had been superfriendly. He'd insisted they have dinner together the first night, had tried to make plans with her for the next day. She'd put him off, telling him she preferred being alone, then had gone and gotten herself involved with Lucky. Adair hadn't been blind to the fact, either.

Some sort of insane jealousy as a motive? That didn't wash, because he hadn't known her before coming to the ranch.

Or had he?

JoJo remembered thinking he looked familiar, and he had admitted to being in Las Vegas for a few days before the movie shoot. Though what that had to do with anything, she didn't know.

Her mind spun with the possibilities, but JoJo found it impossible to draw any certain conclusion, so she slipped back into the hall, thinking she'd better take full advantage of having the house to herself.

Only two rooms left if she cared to search them— Caroline's and Lucky's.

She already knew Caroline better than she wanted to. Lucky's sister had reasons for disliking her. JoJo didn't have to prove that. So what would be the point other than to look for a weapon? Reason enough, she guessed.

But a thorough exploration turned up nothing revealing.

How weird. Caroline had a motive of sorts. But it was Adair who had means and opportunity.

Searching Lucky's room presented JoJo with mixed feelings. On the one hand, the man had saved her life, so she felt she should be able to trust him—she had trusted him enough to make love with him, after all. On the other hand, Eli's telling her about Lucky's going to jail for almost killing a man had jerked her emotions around.

Could Lucky be psychotic, trying to get rid of her with one hand, saving her with the other?

JoJo didn't know what to think...other than being certain that she needed to learn as much about Lucky Donatelli as she could.

Reluctantly, she entered the room that wasn't so different from hers but for the bolder color scheme. Her hands felt like ice, her feet like lead. She wandered about, looking but not touching. After so brazenly searching everyone else's room, she felt doing the same with Lucky's would be an unnecessary invasion of his privacy. Her instincts told her that he meant her no bodily harm.

But she'd been wrong about her instincts before. She'd been too easily duped by Marco Scudella, who'd blinded her with the romance of a whirlwind courtship. He'd been attentive, complimentary and ardent. She'd fallen for the illusion like a babe in the woods.

She'd only known Lucky for four days. Four days of suspicions, altercations and growing lust. How could she be certain that Lucky Donatelli wasn't every bit as dangerous and unscrupulous as her former fiancé?

Confused and feeling too vulnerable, JoJo hesitated at a chair near the door where Lucky had thrown the clothes he'd been wearing earlier. Unable to resist, she picked up his jeans and took a closer look at his belt buckle. In addition to the bull and rider, the buckle declared him to be the World's Champion Bull Rider by the Rodeo Cowboys Association. She traded the jeans for the white T-shirt with the sleeves ripped out. The soft cotton against her fingertips mesmerized her into remembering how the cloth had felt draped over his body.

How his body had felt draped over hers.

JoJo closed her eyes and brought the T-shirt to her cheek, inhaling Lucky's male scent that had surrounded her only hours ago. For a short while lost in the memory of their explosive passion, she was doubly startled by a steely voice that she recognized as his.

"Find everything you need?"

Heart hammering, JoJo dropped the T-shirt. Slowly, keeping control, she turned to face Lucky. "I was just satisfying my curiosity."

"You mean you were snooping."

Caught in the act.

Defensive, she said, "Not a nice word."

"Not a nice thing to do."

Lucky stood in the doorway, shoulder hunched against the jamb, preventing her escape. His features were harsher than usual.

Throat suddenly dry, she contended, "Look who's talking—the man who went through my purse to get my wallet."

"That's different."

"Sure it is."

"I didn't do it behind your back."

JoJo didn't have a return. He was right to be angry. Remorse ate at her. And defiance. Her continued good health—not to mention her life—might be at stake here. Not that she could tell him what she'd been up to for the past hour. Or what she'd found. She'd have to keep her own counsel for a while, until she could figure things out. Self-preservation was more important than a little guilt.

"I'd like to leave now," she said coolly.

He stepped inside the room, his hand on the door as though he intended to close it. "What if I said no?"

"You *are* bigger than me."

"But I don't scare you?" His gaze dropped down to her throat where her pulse jumped.

"Is that what you want?"

His voice husky, he said, "What I want is to hear you cry out again... in the throes of passion."

Lucky's saying it stirred her up inside, made her want the same. He was close, barely a yard away. She could feel the air between them charge. Recognized the instant ache that surged inside her. JoJo fought the sudden lethargy that made her limbs grow weak and her head light. Fought the insistent throbbing between her thighs that reminded her of the tender flesh he'd ravished earlier.

Denying the renewal of desire, she whispered, "Don't hold your breath."

He moved closer. "Don't be so sure you can re-sist." He slid a hand around her neck. "This thing between us is potent." He ran his thumb along the pulse still beating hard against the soft flesh of her throat.

"Stronger than the two of us?" she mocked.

He lifted the hand around her throat slightly, and she automatically rose to her toes. She was aware that he could snap her neck if he so chose....

Or kiss her.

His face was mere inches from hers. So very tempt-ing. Her breath caught in her throat. Her heart thumped against the wall of her chest. Her lips parted. She waited for him to do *something*. When his gray eyes remained flat, she realized he was merely testing her.

Disappointment made her lower her gaze.

As if knowing she recognized his purpose, Lucky opened his hand, releasing her neck. JoJo swayed to-ward him, then caught herself before they touched again. He moved around her without so much as brushing her, as if contact were the last thing he wanted.

Before her, the door stood open, inviting her to leave.

"What are you waiting for?" he asked softly.

As she took the first step, JoJo felt an undeniable sadness well in her. After having been so close only a few hours before, they now should be tender and lov-ing with one another. Not distrustful and sarcastic.

Not hateful.

She turned to him. "I'm sorry." Then hurried out the door before he could reply.

The sound of vehicles pulling up outside warned her the others had returned, and so she raced into her own room and slammed the door. She threw herself across the bed even as voices drifted inside the house. To shut them out, she pulled a pillow over her head.

She was sorry about a lot of things, JoJo thought.

About the emotional state that had brought her here. About the accidents that were no accidents. About the devils that drove Lucky, keeping him from trusting her. About her own inability to trust him.

But she was especially sorry that her affections were getting out of hand, betraying her. For what had started out as simple desire was turning into something far more complex. Something she didn't want to put a name to.

She couldn't be falling in love with Lucky Donatelli.

She just couldn't.

JoJo Weston didn't die easily.

How annoying.

She was a fighter. Tough. Clever.

Of course, the cleverness was no surprise—she'd already proved her ability to keep her head no matter her circumstances well before coming to Arizona. Just as she'd already demonstrated her facility for arousing the male protective instinct.

The trait that had sealed her fate.

Subtlety wasn't working even if nature was cooperating. More-dire measures were called for before the place was swarming with wranglers and new guests.

Time to bring in the reserves.

WAKING UP in the predawn hours the next morning, panicked by dreams of her tryst with Lucky, JoJo couldn't get back to sleep. What had she done? How could she have been so impulsive? *Again.*

She wanted to go home. To Las Vegas. And only one thing stood in her way of doing so…unless they'd caught him, of course. Slipping out of her bedroom, she went straight for the telephone and punched out a Las Vegas number, praying it would be so.

"Deputy Sheriff Ben Carter speaking."

"It's JoJo Weston. Have you found him?"

A big breath on the other end was followed by his "I'm sorry to say Lester Perkins is still at large."

"Isn't anyone looking for him?"

"Every available man and woman."

"Then how could you not find him?" Frustration threatened JoJo's temper. "He escaped on Saturday, for heaven's sake. He's been at large for nearly a week!"

"I can't say, Miss Weston," the deputy said calmly. "It's like he's disappeared. Vanished. We haven't even gotten a lead on him. By now, he could be anywhere."

"Have you checked the Caribbean?" JoJo stared into the dark, remembering. "He held me there in a subbasement. No one goes down there—"

"We already thought of that. No luck."

"I don't understand. Lester's a simple man. How could he elude you for this long? How did he get free to begin with?"

"I guess you'll be reading about it tomorrow, so no harm in telling you. He had help."

"Help?" JoJo's mind raced, but she couldn't visualize Lester with that loyal a friend. "How so?"

"Lester's cell mate Deke kept saying he wanted the new nurse. Only there hasn't been a new nurse in the facility for more than a year. On further questioning, Deke insisted Lester had a new nurse right before he was released."

"Then he had help from the outside."

"That's what we believe."

"What were the guards doing?"

"One of the night guards was on dinner break. The one at the desk was, uh, asleep. He swears something in his coffee musta put him out. Too late to check on that, of course."

A nurse had helped Lester. A vision of Caroline in nurse's whites came automatically to mind. JoJo's grip on the phone was fierce. "Did Deke describe the woman?"

"The supposed nurse was male, Miss Weston. All Deke can remember is that he was big. Deke's pretty heavily medicated at night."

And not very helpful.

JoJo wondered if she'd ever be able to go back to Las Vegas.

"TLAQUEPAQUE IS the coolest shopping center I've ever seen," Paula maintained the next morning as she drove JoJo into Sedona. "It's a replica of a Mexican village near Guadalajara, though of course it's nicer than the original, being that it's newer and all. Wait till you see the plazas and fountains and sculptures. It even has a bell tower. Good thing the rain stopped, since it's an outdoor center. The shops are to die for— clothes, jewelry, furnishings, art. You name it and they sell it. And we'll have several nice restaurants to choose from for lunch."

Paula chatted on in her usual motor-mouth style. She described several of the shops and their wares in detail. JoJo nodded and made small sounds that assured the other woman she was all ears.

In truth, she was only half listening, and glad to be removed from the ranch even if for a few hours. Maybe away from Lucky, she'd get her head back on straight. At the very least, she'd get some relief from his looming—and silent—presence. By the time they'd finished breakfast, she'd been ready to crawl up the wall with wondering what he was thinking.

"Hey, would you mind changing the music?" Paula asked, bumping into JoJo's reverie. "The case of CDs is behind my seat."

"Sure."

Not that she'd even realized the music was on. A CD player, instead of the more typical audiocassette, another example of Paula's costly preferences. Thinking about audiotapes reminded JoJo of the Bushwhacker incident. Which made her a bit clumsy as she pulled the case from the floor. The leather slipped from her fingers, and she heard the bounce of plastic.

"Oops. Dropped something." She tried hiking herself around despite her seat belt. "I can't see what, though."

"No prob. I'll get it later," Paula said with a wave of her beringed hand.

JoJo unzipped the bag. "What are you in the mood for?"

"Anything but another Beethoven. I feel like I've been listening to the same CD for thousands of miles, ever since I left home."

Certain that was an exaggeration, since Phoenix was barely more than a hundred miles away, JoJo glanced through the CDs—mostly classical music. "Liszt okay?"

"Fine."

JoJo changed CDs, settled back in her seat and stared out the window as they approached Sedona. The sky was a brilliant blue against the red rock. The earth was dry, the sandy soil having absorbed every lick of water left by the storm. If she didn't know better, she could believe it hadn't rained at all in days.

"What do you think of Rocky?" Paula asked suddenly.

"In what way?"

"He's a babe, right?"

"I hadn't noticed."

Paula laughed. "You've been too busy eyeballing Lucky." She shivered. "Those scars make him look too mean for me."

JoJo felt her hackles rise at the criticism. "I don't judge anyone by their looks."

"Baloney. It's human nature." Paula gave her a wide-eyed scrutiny. "It's just that different women like different men. Thank goodness."

"I take that to mean you're interested in Rocky and you want an all-clear signal."

"Well...you spent so much time with him yesterday on the trail, I just wondered."

"Don't worry. I'm not interested."

"Good." Paula grinned and turned into a parking lot. "Here we are."

A moment later, they were parked and on their way to the nearest entrance. Wanting to make certain she remembered where the car was in case they were separated, JoJo glanced back for the location and license number. Her first good look at Paula's license plate told her the car was a rental. How odd. JoJo put it to Paula's divorce. Maybe she'd been left without a car. Or maybe she had an older model she didn't trust for a long drive through the desert. Whichever, JoJo didn't want to embarrass the woman, so she didn't ask.

Paula proved to be a charming and distracting companion as she led JoJo from one store to the next through a series of courtyards. A person could get turned around pretty quickly in the maze, and without a map, JoJo feared she wouldn't be able to find her way back to the parking lot, no less the car. She should be paying more attention, but she was content to let someone else do the brain work.

A soothing breeze blew over her, sending lilting tinkles her way. "I love wind chimes."

"Why don't you go look?" Paula said. "I'll be in the jewelry shop next door."

JoJo discovered both the unusual wind chimes and bells were designed by Soleri, an unorthodox architect. The unique souvenirs supported an ongoing project located in the desert on the road to Phoenix. JoJo impulsively chose to buy one of his smaller concrete-and-metal bells, thinking she'd place it in her kitchen window.

She was exiting the shop, package under her arm, when she felt as if someone were watching her. She turned quickly, but spotted no familiar face in the throng of tourists behind her. Still, she couldn't shake the feeling as she found Paula, who immediately distracted her long enough to drag her across another courtyard.

To JoJo's surprise, Paula put off making any purchases, though she admired Sadie Buckthorn earrings similar to her ring in one shop, a tuxedo blouse with crystal saguaro cactus buttons in another and a lovely glazed pot in iridescent colors in a third—all very expensive items.

"I can't believe you're not buying anything," JoJo commented when they came out of yet another shop, Paula empty-handed.

"This vacation is a credit-card luxury I can't really afford," she admitted with a sigh. "I needed some time away, though, to get over...things. I'd rather have some fun to occupy my mind than go into therapy."

Even if she hadn't actually married Marco, JoJo could identify with the emotional upheaval of a breakup. She didn't have long to think about it, however, for in what had to be the farthest corner of Tlaquepaque, a camera crew was just breaking down its equipment. JoJo stared. A few costumed actors were talking to a man in jeans and ragged sweater. Some tourists were standing around and watching, but it was obvious the excitement was over.

Paula gave the small group an uninterested onceover. "I want to check out some prices. Coming?"

Transfixed by the movie company, JoJo said, "I think I'll wait out here."

"I'll be quick."

JoJo wandered closer to the small group, and when a dark-haired young woman looked up from her equipment box and smiled at her, asked, "Is this the *Call of the West* shoot?"

The brunette nodded. "Our last day."

"I met one of your stuntmen. Adair Keating."

Her brow furrowed. "I don't recognize the name."

"Tall, gorgeous, blond haired and blue eyed."

"Sounds like someone I couldn't forget."

But JoJo could see the brunette didn't remember him. "He's pretty unforgettable, all right."

"Not one of our stuntmen." The young woman gave her a sympathetic look. "I guess he was trying to impress you."

"Maybe. Thanks."

If Adair wasn't who he said he was . . . then who exactly was he, and why had he thought it necessary to lie?

"I'm back," Paula announced, "and I'm starving. Let's go eat."

Over lunch, JoJo encouraged Paula to talk about the divorce and her feelings, but for once, the other woman wasn't forthcoming. She didn't have much to say either about her ex-husband or the breakup, and JoJo couldn't help wondering if Paula wasn't being purposely vague. No doubt, she was eager to forget the stressful details and was putting on a happy facade to boot.

So, instead, over stuffed *poblano* peppers on polenta cakes, JoJo once more found herself answering questions about her own career, Paula seeming to be more interested in her Broadway years than the past few months in Las Vegas.

"I always think of Broadway as being so glamorous and exciting. All the attention from the media. And plenty of stage-door Johnnies, right?"

The woman really was obsessed with men. Amused, JoJo said, "Usually when you didn't even want them."

"You didn't meet anyone worthwhile?"

"One man."

Thoughts of Oliver reminded JoJo about the letter from his lawyers that she still hadn't read through. When she got back to the ranch . . .

With long purple nails, Paula scraped her hair behind one ear. "And you let him get away?"

"We were just good friends."

"Then you weren't in love with him?"

"No." An image of Lucky flashed through JoJo's mind, but she pushed it away.

"What about *him?*" Paula asked. "Are you sure he wasn't in love with you?"

"There are all kinds of love."

"Some that just won't fade, even with time."

JoJo shifted uncomfortably. She didn't want to think that any feelings she might have for Lucky would haunt her. She had enough baggage to carry around with her as it was.

JoJo chose to turn the focus on Paula. "Is that how you feel about your ex?"

But as had happened earlier, Paula didn't seem too forthcoming. "I have regrets, but I'm not going to let them stop me from getting what I want."

"A practical viewpoint."

"A girl's got to be practical. She's got to look out for herself." Paula's baby blues bore into JoJo. "You agree with that, don't you?"

JoJo did, if not in exactly the same way as Paula. "As long as it doesn't hurt someone else."

Paula shrugged. "Sometimes hurting someone else can't be helped."

Not wanting to continue the discussion, JoJo purposely changed the subject, telling a couple of amusing stories about her life with Sasha as a roommate.

Paula didn't seem to be too interested in hearing about another woman, however, and after quickly finishing her lunch, she excused herself to find the ladies' room. While she was gone, JoJo signaled the waitress and asked for their bill.

And realized they'd soon be heading back to the ranch.

And Lucky.

Telling Paula about Sasha had made JoJo miss her best friend. If only she could pick up the phone and talk to her, ask for her advice. If she could even talk to Nick about his brother, find out what Lucky was really like under all that old anger. Maybe her two friends could help her sort out her feelings for Lucky one way or the other.

Maybe Nick could assure her that his brother had no taste for violence.

Though where she was concerned, someone did.

A furtive movement from the corner of her eye sent JoJo spinning in her chair, but before she could spot the source of her discomfort, the waitress arrived with the bill and blocked her line of sight. Feeling badly that Paula was flat broke, JoJo decided to spring for lunch. After all, she wasn't even paying to stay at the ranch, so she could afford to treat the other woman. Still feeling jumpy, she glanced around her as she dug into her purse. Nothing was out of place.

The waitress was just leaving with the money when Paula returned to the table.

"Oops. I don't have cash to give you back. I was going to put the bill on plastic."

"My treat."

"Really? Thanks. I'll get the next one." Smiling, Paula slipped into her chair and finished her ice tea. "It's been a fun morning, hasn't it?"

"A lot less eventful than yesterday."

"You and Lucky were kind of vague about what happened."

JoJo kept her voice light when she said, "I was on foot when I got caught in the flash flood through that wash we crossed, and was nearly swept away."

"Swept away... and not by a man." Paula giggled. "Tsk-tsk. What a waste."

Of course, the conversation would revert to men. She *had* been swept away by Lucky for a short while, JoJo remembered. If only those feelings could have lasted...

"I don't mean to make light of the situation," Paula added. "It's just that I don't deal well with death."

"Me, neither. But I am unscathed, so there's a happy ending to this story."

"Happy endings are important." Her expression serious, Paula said, "I'm looking forward to one of my own, and soon."

Meaning she was on the hunt for a replacement husband? JoJo wondered. She remembered their earlier conversation. Rocky didn't seem like the best husband material, but you never knew what other people looked for in a lifetime mate.

They left the restaurant and started across one of the courtyards when Paula suddenly stopped. "Oh, heck, I forgot to make a phone call. You want to wait here for a minute or meet me back at the car?"

Figuring she'd be lucky to find her way back to the correct parking lot since she'd relied on the other woman to lead her around the maze of shops all morning, JoJo thought she'd better stay put. She spotted a nearby souvenir emporium.

"I could use some postcards. I'll be over there."

"See you in a few," Paula said, already off.

As she chose portraits of Sedona's magnificent red rocks to send to her mother, brother and Sasha and Nick—even knowing she might get back to Las Vegas before the newlyweds did—JoJo grew increasingly uncomfortable. She fought the feeling that crept up on her every time she was alone.

The feeling of being watched.

She handed the clerk money for her postcards and, while waiting for her change, glanced around. No one seemed in the least bit interested in her.

"Here you go, miss."

Startled, JoJo turned to see the clerk holding out her purchases and change. "Thanks."

Wandering back into the courtyard, she slipped the coins into a pocket. She was inserting the small bag with her cards into the bell bag when she felt it again.

Someone *was* watching her.

Her pulse picked up and her mouth went dry. She felt every bit as skittish as on the morning of the wedding. She had reason to be wary, she assured herself. To make herself feel better, she gave everyone around her a thorough inspection. No vibes, and yet the feeling didn't fade with reassurance. She was tense, wound tight as a spring.

What was taking Paula so long?

And where exactly had the other woman gone to make her phone call?

JoJo tried distracting herself. She sauntered from store to store, window to window, stopping before each to give the displayed goods a once-over. With each passing minute, her nerves wound tighter. When she realized she wasn't registering what was directly before her eyes, her gaze strayed upward to the windowpane itself.

And caught the reflection in the glass.

He was thin as ever, too-big clothes hanging loose on his bony frame. His glasses sat crookedly on the tip of his nose. He punched at them, and they bobbled precariously.

Her heart stilled. Her mouth went dry. JoJo thought she was either going to throw up or faint.

She blinked hard, willing the image to disappear, but it didn't so much as fade.

Even knowing she had to get out of there, she couldn't make her legs work. Her limbs felt as solid as two rubber bands, and her knees were shaking. She held on to her bags as hard as she could and pushed herself off anyway. Stumbling across the courtyard, she looked around wildly, wondering which of two exits to take.

She had to get out of there, had to get someplace safe.

But where was safe from a man as obsessed as Lester Perkins?

Chapter Ten

"JoJo, wait!" Lester yelled from somewhere behind her.

JoJo didn't pause. Stomach turning, she ran faster. As she shot through a plaza and skirted a multitiered fountain, she knocked into a teenager.

"Hey, lady! Watch where you're going!" the angry kid yelled after her.

Blind with panic, JoJo didn't hesitate long enough to apologize.

"JoJo, stop!" came Lester's voice again.

She didn't turn to look for him. She couldn't let him catch up to her. She had to get away.

Lester Perkins wasn't mentally stable. She'd known that when he'd held her captive for nearly a week—according to him, *for her own good*. Not that he'd hurt her. But then he had become the prisoner, and somehow he'd escaped. And now he'd found her. Why?

What was going through his warped mind?

Practically flying, she chanced a glance over her shoulder. Lester had fallen behind, was held up by a family of tourists. Awkwardly, he tried to struggle free. Fear lent speed to her feet, and she zoomed around a corner, looking wildly for someplace safe to hide.

There was no place safe from Lester, an inner voice warned her.

JoJo took refuge anyway in a public rest room, whipping inside, leaning her back against a cool tile wall and clutching her package to her breast. Sweat trickled down her face and ran down her neck, and she was gasping for air. Several women at the sinks and in line for stalls gave her odd looks. Though she was distracted, she noticed their interest and grew increasingly uncomfortable.

Shaking inside, JoJo moved to an unoccupied sink. She set her package on a shelf and poured cool water over her wrists. Then she cupped her hands and rinsed off her face and neck, as well. The simple act was comforting, but, of course, she couldn't get Lester out of her mind.

His showing up in Sedona was no coincidence—he'd come after her, no doubt in revenge for being put into a psychiatric ward.

Had he been the one all along, then? The one orchestrating the accidents?

She could easily believe that he'd been able to get his hands on a tape of the music from the show. But how he'd learned of her whereabouts, and how he'd gotten from Las Vegas to Sedona were harder to imagine.

Where Lester was concerned, anything was possible, JoJo reminded herself.

What to do?

She had to inform the authorities. But first, she'd have to leave the shelter of the ladies' room. The thought made her take a deep breath so she wouldn't be sick. Lester could be out there, waiting for her. He could have a weapon. Alone, she would be a target. But if she involved other people, they could be hurt, as well.

In the end, she chose to leave surreptitiously a small distance behind two women who were so absorbed in their conversation that they didn't notice her. Mouth dry, palms sweaty, she kept a vigilant eye out for Lester and clutched at her package as if it were a lifeline.

Once out in the courtyard, she spotted a telephone, but a big, burly man was using it. She dared not wait, dared not expose herself. She kept moving with the crowd, skirting along the shops rather than cutting through the open center, hoping she could find another phone on the way to the car. No doubt, Paula would be waiting for her in the parking lot. At least, she assumed the other woman would figure she'd gone back to the car as suggested.

Head turning, gaze constantly searching every corner of the shopping center for any sign of Lester, JoJo stumbled on, pulse thrumming strangely, encouraged when she recognized a sculpture she and Paula had passed earlier that morning. She advanced through and into another familiar courtyard and figured she was now in the vicinity of the correct parking lot.

Almost home free.

A glance around assured her Lester was nowhere in sight. But another telephone was. And this one wasn't in use. She hesitated . . . and a hand hooked her arm. JoJo shrieked and spun around, throwing her package like a weapon.

With a grunt, Lucky caught it in the gut. "If you wanted me to hold this, you could have just asked."

"It's you!" JoJo's head was spinning. "My God, did you have to scare me like that? Why do you always *do* that?" she demanded even as she realized she'd never been so glad to see anyone in her life. "I've got to call the police." But when she turned back toward the telephone, she saw a teenager was already picking up the receiver. "Damn!"

"Hey, what's going on?" Expression concerned, Lucky stared at her. "Someone steal your wallet?"

"No." Not knowing what else to do, JoJo headed for the archway that would take her to the parking lot. She'd call the police from the safety of the ranch. "I have to find Paula. What are you doing here anyway?"

"Looking for you. You're going in the wrong direction." Placing a hand in the middle of her back, he steered her toward a different exit. "I ran into Paula in the parking lot—she didn't know where you were."

As they passed through the opening, JoJo took a last look over her shoulder, almost expecting to see Lester standing there, glasses bobbling on the tip of his nose, his thin body tensed in frustration.

But he'd vanished.

For now.

In the opposite direction, Paula leaned against the hood of her car, engrossed in a conversation with Eli until she spotted JoJo. Then she straightened and waved. Relieved that the torture of the past few days was almost over—that Lester would soon be in custody—JoJo grinned weakly and waved back.

A moment later, she was taking her purchase from Lucky and placing it on the rear seat of the car. Straightening, JoJo caught a flash of silver-and-purple gemstone at Paula's ear, and realized she'd bought the

Sadie Buckthorn earrings she supposedly couldn't afford.

Before JoJo could comment on the purchase, Paula asked, "Where'd you disappear to?"

"It's a long story."

"One I want to hear," Lucky said, steering her away from the passenger door. "Eli, do you mind riding with Paula?"

"No problem."

Paula looked surprised but offered no protest. And the next thing JoJo knew, she was settled in Lucky's Bronco. She wondered why he waited until they were on the road to start his interrogation.

"So give."

"I think I know why I've been having such bad luck lately. Lester Perkins."

"Lester...you're not talking about the same Lester Perkins who used to—"

"Work for your father," JoJo finished for him. "One and the same."

"He was always a harmless soul."

"He killed Mia Scudella."

"I don't believe it."

"Welcome back to the real world, Lucky." JoJo stared out at the landscape that looked like a movie set. Or one that had been made into a movie set, she amended, reminded of Adair's false claim to being a stuntman on the shoot. "You've been gone too long."

Lucky took a moment to digest this. "All right, say he did kill Mia. What does that have to do with you?"

"Lester identified himself with your brother. He'd had a thing for Mia, probably because Nick was engaged to her. Lester told Mia he cared for her, and she laughed at him. I don't think he meant to, but he did kill her. As you know, he got away with murder for years. Who would suspect him? Lester was working for Nick when he hired me as a dancer. I was always friendly to Lester, and he took it for more, especially when Nick and I hung out together.''

''You're saying he had a thing for you like he did for Mia?''

''Enough to take me prisoner rather than let me marry the man I knew as Mac Schneider. Lester was certain he was evil—he may even have known Mac was really Marco. He locked me up because he was afraid for me.''

''Then why do you think he's responsible for what's been happening to you?''

JoJo leaned her head against the side window. Her adrenaline was fading fast, leaving her exhausted, both physically and emotionally.

''He may blame me for his being locked up in a psychiatric ward,'' she told Lucky. ''He escaped the morning of Nick and Sasha's wedding. Didn't Caroline tell you when she was going on about my relationship with Marco?''

''Not a word.''

How surprising. Undoubtedly, his sister had given him a carefully edited version of the truth so as to put JoJo in the worst light possible.

''Lester made his way to Sedona somehow,'' JoJo explained. ''He followed me to Tlaquepaque and waited until I was alone to get to me.''

''He threatened you with all those people around?''

''I didn't let him close enough.'' JoJo started when she realized Lucky had a cellular phone in his Bronco. Wishing he'd tell her he believed her story and that she wasn't working for his father, she started to pick up the phone.

He put his hand over hers. "Don't call the police."

"Why not?"

"I've known Lester all my life. He may be sick, but he's not evil."

"I didn't say he was."

"With the police involved, anything could happen. He might be killed. Let me handle this. I'll find Lester and bring him in."

Not knowing what to say, JoJo stared at Lucky. She didn't want to see Lester Perkins dead, either, even if he had tried to kill her out of revenge for his being locked up. But how did Lucky think he could find Lester? The man could be holed up anywhere, even in one of the nearby canyons. She didn't care to believe that Lucky didn't want Lester found, but her suspicions were engaged yet again.

Letting go of Lucky's phone as if agreeing to let him handle the situation alone, JoJo wished she could read his mind.

What *had* Lucky been doing at Tlaquepaque? And with Eli? The glitzy tourist shopping center didn't appear to be their sort of place.

Then again, Lucky always seemed to show up directly after something unexpected and unpleasant happened to her.

The Bushwhacker incident.

The flash flood.

And now Lester.

Did Lucky already know where Lester was?

JoJo couldn't decide if Lucky was her hero or a man more clever and dangerous than any she'd ever met. A male nurse had helped Lester escape. A big man.

Lucky? He could be using her to get back at his father.

A sick thought, one that chilled JoJo, especially since she'd made it so easy for him. She'd fallen into his arms right on cue. And now her emotions were all tangled up in little knots where he was concerned. She could deny the facts all she wanted, but she felt more for Lucky Donatelli than a healthy dose of desire called for.

Swallowing the lump that stuck in her throat, she asked, "So what *were* you doing at Tlaquepaque—other than looking for me?"

"Seeing a man about business."

What man? Lester? JoJo shook the evil thought away. Too complicated to be true. She was fabricating. Paranoid.

"Anything you care to talk about?" she asked, hoping he would give her a reason to have faith in him.

"Not yet."

And that was the end of that conversation, JoJo realized, suppressing her disappointment.

They were nearing the Macbride property. She only hoped that, once there, Lucky wouldn't stick to her like glue. The moment she got inside the house, she intended on making a phone call to Las Vegas.

A call that Lucky would undoubtedly stop if he could.

"SO WHAT'S UP, LUCKY?" Eli asked as they headed for the outbuildings a few minutes after arriving at the ranch. "With the woman, I mean."

Lucky glanced back, but JoJo was already inside the house with Paula. He was wound tight as a spring over the situation—Lester's complicating everything—but he wasn't about to share that with his friend. What was happening between him and JoJo was eating at him. He had plans. He didn't need complications. He didn't need to worry that he could be wrong about being able to handle Lester.

He should have stayed away from JoJo the moment he'd suspected she was his father's creature. Rather than taunting her, trying to drive her out, he should have moved into the Wrangler's Roost with Eli.

Out of sight, out of mind.

She'd be gone soon enough, Lucky realized, and he knew damn well he wouldn't easily forget her. Maybe if he hadn't held her in his arms and made love to her, he'd be relieved to see her go. As it was, he was torn about her leaving. Part of him wanted to throw her a parade to see her off. Part of him wanted to force her to stay.

No woman had ever tied him up in knots like this before, and Lucky wasn't liking it one bit.

"Hey, you on some different planet, or what?" Eli asked.

Lucky realized he still hadn't told him anything. He carefully studied his friend's expression when he said, "Lester Perkins." No hint of recognition.

Eli shrugged. "Wanna be more specific?"

"Lester's worked for my family all his life. He's...slow. And kind of odd. He got himself in deep trouble recently and landed in a psychiatric ward. A few days ago, he escaped. And now he's here."

"You see him yourself?"

"He saw JoJo. Put her into a panic." Lucky suspected she was far more freaked than she'd let on.

"You're not gonna involve the cops?"

Eli's aversion to the authorities was no secret, not to mention perfectly understandable, so Lucky didn't get uptight at the question. "I'm planning on getting to Lester myself."

"Then what?"

"I haven't decided."

"DID YOU AND LUCKY HAVE an interesting ride home?" Paula asked, throwing her legs over one arm of an upholstered chair, wedging her back against the other.

"The same ride you did."

"Now, why do I doubt that?"

"True," JoJo said, relaxing into the couch cushions. "Eli is more civilized."

Paula laughed. "You have a thing for Lucky, don't you?"

"He does have a definite effect on me."

"What more could a girl ask for?" Paula sighed. "So what shall we do till dinner? We could take the horses out again. Or how about a hike around one of the vortexes?"

"You may have the energy, but I'm beat." She'd probably used up all her adrenaline for the next week. "I just need some quiet time."

Time without Paula, JoJo thought, sliding a glance across the room toward the phone. In the house for nearly a quarter of an hour and not a second to herself. She wanted to make that call, but with some privacy. The call could wait a bit longer.

"We could kick back and talk."

About men? That's where all of Paula's conversations led, it seemed. Thinking she could go to her room and have some time to herself, JoJo was about to say she needed a real lie down when the front door opened and Rocky burst through, followed by Adair and Caroline.

"So, did you girls buy up Sedona?" Adair asked.

"Not today," Paula said.

"There's always tomorrow."

"Man, I'm bushed," Rocky complained, his legs a bit bowed as he wobbled to the couch. He sprawled at the end opposite JoJo.

"Another horseback ride?" Paula asked.

"Nah. We were learning to rope."

"Rope what?"

"Livestock, of course."

"Pretend livestock," Caroline amended.

"There's a wooden bull with a real skull set up over by the enclosure," Adair explained. "Vincent said that's the way rodeo cowboys practice roping."

"I'm all roped out," Rocky said with a yawn.

And JoJo realized she wasn't going to get the privacy she was looking for, especially not with Caroline settling herself in the kitchen right next to the cordless phone. Maybe it was a sign that she should forget about calling the Las Vegas authorities.

"I think I'll go take a look at the new killer bull," JoJo joked as she got to her feet.

"You wouldn't want company, would you?" Adair asked. "I can give you instructions."

JoJo didn't miss Caroline's sudden sour expression. "I can figure it out for myself." She had no desire to be alone with him anyway.

If her rebuff had any effect on Adair, he didn't show it, but merely poked his head in the fridge. JoJo left the ranch house, glad to be alone for a while. As she strolled across the property, she thought about Lucky and his plea that she let him find Lester himself. She still didn't know whether or not to trust the man.

Either she was going to believe in him or she wasn't. Her choice. And a fine fix, considering all that had happened to her over the past few months. She'd believed in Mac/Marco, and look where blind trust had gotten her. Maybe that was the problem—the past wasn't quite the past yet. And until she resolved her part in a relationship that had led to her kidnapping, she would probably hold any man who attracted her in suspicion.

Maybe she just didn't trust her own instincts.

So she'd made a mistake. Time to get over it. Time to start anew. Judge a man for his own worth, not compare him to another. Just because Lucky and Marco were both sons of crime bosses didn't mean they were cut from the same cloth. And she had to remember that if Lucky had wanted her permanently out of the way, he wouldn't have saved her from the gully washer.

Besides which, he would have needed a great deal of foresight—or rather second sight—to free Lester Perkins to get to her. At the time, he wouldn't have known she was coming to Sedona, because she herself hadn't. So he couldn't have engineered some complex plot against his father involving her—she was just certain of it. At worst, he'd tried driving her off the ranch from day one by showing her his devil side, because he and Eli had something to hide.

But someone had engineered a plot specifically against her. Someone had sprung Lester. *Some big man.* Adair?

The conclusion was logical. She'd already suspected Adair anyway. He had a gun. And now she knew for certain that he'd lied about being a stunt-man on *Call of the West.*

Adair's being at the ranch with witnesses when Lester came after her meant nothing, JoJo reasoned. Lester was off kilter, but he wasn't a child. He was perfectly capable of taking care of himself, of responding to a phone call telling him where she'd be and when.

But if Adair *were* pulling Lester's strings, she still had one unanswerable question—why? What had she ever done to earn his enmity? Could the two men be related? Not that Lester had ever told her anything about family. Of course, it was possible that Lester was working alone here. Not likely, considering the circumstances, but possible.

If only she could go to the authorities. She *should* call them, despite Lucky's plea. But she felt sorry for Lester, and in truth, didn't want the poor man hurt or worse. She'd press Lucky for his plan of action and then decide.

JoJo was within yards of the outbuildings when she realized Lucky had beat her there. He and Eli were near Bushwhacker's enclosure, looped ropes in hand. Vincent was there, too, his brow furrowing and head nodding as Lucky spoke. Then he jogged off, and JoJo realized a tacked-up horse waited for Vincent nearby. The wrangler rode in the direction of the grazing lands where Flora had told her the Macbride crew was headed with the rounded-up strays.

No sooner had she spotted the wooden bull than Lucky's rope whipped up into the air, whirling around his head...stretching out in front of him...and looping directly around the bull's neck. Eli was next, his throw equally successful. The men retrieved their ropes and returned to their lassoing positions. JoJo figured the men might be there for some time.

And the Wrangler's Roost would be empty.

Never having been inside the place, JoJo thought to satisfy her curiosity. Eli was staying there. And she suspected that when Lucky disappeared to "work" with Eli, that's where they holed up. Wanting to know exactly what they'd been laboring over, she silently stole away, waiting until the men were out of sight before breaking into a jog.

A few minutes later, she was at the entrance of the original ranch house, a log cabin with several additions. The front door was unlocked. Even so, when she stepped inside, she called, "Anyone home?" and waited a moment. Just in case.

The deserted main room was a smaller version of that in the new house. It had wood-paneled walls and a stone fireplace. In addition to sitting and eating areas, however, a corner space provided for a large work area, as well—a desk and a long table undoubtedly meant for the foreman's use. But the foreman was out on the range, and it was evident that the area had been utilized quite recently if the mugs and the lingering smell of coffee were any indication.

JoJo investigated. Pinned to the table was a layout of what appeared to be a resort. On closer inspection, she realized she was looking at a two-dimensional view of the Macbride Ranch, with additional buildings and stock areas sketched in. Curious. Nick hadn't said anything about changes.

Then, maybe Nick didn't know about this.

The first clue that she was caught snooping came with the opening of the front door. She and Eli were equally surprised to see each other. At least he didn't have a reason to be embarrassed.

Heat crawling up her neck, JoJo tried to save face. "I was looking for Lucky."

"He ain't here."

"So I see."

Eli crossed to the work corner and eyed the plans. "Lucky said you were nosy."

"If you didn't want anyone to see this, you shouldn't have left it out."

"It's not me who's gonna be mad."

Knowing Eli wasn't about to keep her visit a secret, JoJo asked, "Why would Lucky be angry?"

"Talk to him about that."

"Sometimes it's hard to talk to Lucky about anything."

"He does have a temper."

"So I've noticed." A really bad temper, from what Eli had told her before, the comment having shaken her feelings for him. JoJo had to know. "Did he really try to kill a man with his bare hands?"

"Lucky admits to it. From what I heard, that bastard Bob Ray Wyatt deserved a pounding and worse."

"Why? What did he do?"

"Mistreated at least one of his animals. Lucky caught him taking a rubber hose to his horse over losing a team roping competition."

"How horrible," she whispered, grabbing on to the back of a chair.

"Poor old guy was tied down so he couldn't get away, and the bastard was working him over, opening his flesh good. Lucky came runnin' when he heard the horse's screams. He figured that Bob Ray oughta know what a rubber hose felt like on *his* flesh. The bastard hung on to that weapon tubing for all he was worth, so Lucky tried tearing him apart with his hands. I guess he did a fair job of it. He said every day he spent in that cell was worth it.''

The story sickened JoJo... and gave her the bit of faith in Lucky that she'd been looking for. If she'd had any doubts left, they had just disappeared. A man who'd put himself on the line to protect an animal like that couldn't mean her harm.

"What happened to the horse?" she asked fearfully, hoping the poor creature hadn't died of the wounds.

"Lucky bought him—Silverado. Ain't never been a nag more grateful, neither.''

JoJo remembered noticing the scars. "He does have a way with horses." *And women.* At least one woman, she thought, so relieved that she could hardly stand it. "I hope this Bob Ray isn't allowed anywhere near animals again.''

"Lots of things should or shouldn't be," Eli said. "Doesn't mean that's the way things are, though." He glanced out the window. "There's Lucky now."

JoJo caught a glimpse of him through the window herself. Her pulse lurched and she took a deep breath, steeling herself for a confrontation. It was as if Lucky sensed her presence, even through the thick walls of the house, for the moment he opened the door, he pinned her with that disconcerting flat gray gaze.

"Lady's been lookin' for you," Eli said.

"Well, now she's found me."

"I need to get on that *business* we talked about, so I'll leave you two be."

"Thanks, Eli," JoJo said, referring to his sharing the story about Lucky.

Eli tipped his hat to her and slid out the front door.

JoJo shifted her gaze to Lucky. Something seemed different about him. Or maybe it was just the way she was viewing him . . . through new eyes.

"I'm surprised to see you out and around," he said, moving closer. "After your scare with Lester, I'd have thought you'd take to your room with a sick headache or something."

"You don't know me very well or you'd realize I'm not the type of woman who has *or somethings.*"

He stopped mere inches from her before asking, "Exactly what type of woman are you, JoJo Weston?"

"One that you can trust, Lucky Donatelli." She wished more than anything that he could believe her.

"Is that why you're nosing around here?" With a menacing expression, he reached out a hand, knuckling the slant of her jaw. "To prove I can trust you?"

She ignored his suspicions. Wanting to get even closer, she moved her cheek against his fingers and watched his expression dissolve into one of bewilderment.

"I was a little curious," she said.

"About what?"

"You."

"You know all you need to know about me."

"I've barely broken the surface," she argued, a little breathless. "But I'm getting there."

Lucky whipped his hand away from her. His jaw clenched and unclenched, and JoJo figured he was warring with himself as to whether or not her interest was personal or paid for. If he wanted to believe she was acting on Sally's behalf, she could say nothing to convince him otherwise. He would have to make up his mind about her—just as she had about him—based on what he'd learned of her, added to his own gut instinct. He would have to trust her or not. Trust couldn't be forced.

Blood thrumming through her at an accelerated pace, she pried herself away from him, moved toward the worktable. "So what was the business Eli had to take care of?"

"You're not going to let it alone, are you?"

"It's about this, right?" she asked, running the pads of her fingers along the proposed plan of the ranch. "All those new buildings sketched in. The big new barn. Why? What's it all mean?"

JoJo turned to face Lucky and realized he was frozen where she'd left him, his gaze intent on her. Knowing his fear was that the knowledge was meant for his father, she willed him to look into her heart.

"I couldn't go on like I was," he finally said. "I had to settle somewhere. The ranch wasn't making it anymore, not even taking in guests. I thought to turn the place into more of a profit maker."

"By converting it into a resort?"

"By expanding on the idea Nick and Caroline and I came up with a dozen years ago. A working ranch that caters to tourists, only with a little more flair and a lot more fun—like adding weekly rodeos with participation events for the guests. I'm willing to put lots of elbow grease into the deal to make Mama's legacy into a paying proposition. It's all a dream right now, because I don't have the expansion capital. Yet."

"I don't understand. Even if *you* don't have it, Caroline and Nick—"

"That's *family* money—exactly what I'm trying to avoid. I want to work a deal with Nick and Caroline, make them silent partners. This would be my venture with capital I scrape together myself.''

He had to trust her a little to tell her so much. Inordinately happy, she was content to leave it alone for the moment and change the subject. "I've been thinking about Lester."

"I told you to leave him to me."

"Do you have a plan?"

"I'm working on it. In the meantime, I sent Vincent out to the range. He'll bring back a few men I'll put on guard to protect you."

She took a big breath. "Lester's not the only one we have to worry about."

Her statement took him by surprise. "What's that?"

"Someone helped him escape. I think that someone is a paying guest."

"Who?"

"Adair's been awfully interested in me since he arrived. He would have been my shadow if I'd let him. He's no stuntman—at least not on *Call of the West* like he's been telling everyone. And he's keeping a handgun under his... in one of his drawers," she finished, thinking better than to mention the silk underwear.

"You've been real busy checking him out."

JoJo lifted her eyebrows at Lucky's chagrined tone. "Checking out everyone," she assured him. "But everything points to Adair."

"What's he got against you?"

"I don't have a clue," she admitted. "Closest I could figure is that he and Lester are related."

Lucky shook his head. "Lester never had anyone that I knew of." He clucked to himself. "So, not only do I have to track down a man with a few screws loose,

I have to figure out a way of taking care of one who's armed and dangerous.''

"*If* he's the one, you'll have to set a trap for them both.'' JoJo wasn't thrilled by the prospect of what she was about to propose, but she knew her only other choice was to notify the authorities. "Using *me* as the bait.''

Chapter Eleven

"I'm not letting you put yourself in more danger!" Lucky insisted.

Which made JoJo stare in wonderment. He sounded as if he cared what happened to her...maybe cared *for* her just a little, even if he'd been acting otherwise since they'd made love. Her smile warred with his glare.

"You don't have a choice," she said. "*We* don't have a choice. At least this time, I'll have some warning, and hopefully I'll have control of the situation."

But Lucky wasn't so easily swayed. "The situation can turn ugly fast."

"I'll chance it."

"I don't want to chance—"

"What?" she asked breathlessly, willing him to add *losing you.*

"Having something go wrong," he said instead. "You get yourself killed, and how many tourists do you think would set foot on the Macbride Ranch?"

If he was trying to make her angry, he'd succeeded. JoJo fumed and fisted a hand so she wouldn't smack him. "Probably lots of them! People love the macabre," she informed him, poking her face practically into his. "You could make an attraction of my death!"

"Don't talk like that!"

"Why not? You've been wanting to be rid of me since you laid eyes on me!"

He scowled. "I don't want anything bad to happen to you."

"Why not?" she pressed.

He backed up a bit. "I wouldn't want anything bad to happen to anyone I know."

"Is that it?" JoJo wouldn't let him off the hook so easily. "Cut-and-dried?" Eyes wide, she placed the flat of her hand on his chest. "Nothing personal?" She could feel his heartbeat speed up under her hand. His nostrils flared, and an emotion other than anger flashed through his eyes. She took a chance. Stepped closer. "Are you sure you don't feel anything personal for me at all?"

With a groan, Lucky grabbed her upper arms and pulled her flat against him, the action so taut, her neck snapped. That only put her head at the proper angle, she realized as his mouth crashed down over hers.

JoJo slipped both hands up, twining them around the back of his neck. She'd been wanting this ever since they returned to the ranch after the rain. Lucky's arms wrapped around her back, his heat encasing her like a blanket. His tongue thrust past her lips to possess her mouth. She welcomed him gladly. Took in his tongue with the same passion she had the rest of him when they'd made love the day before.

For a moment, she reveled in the sensations created by his hands as they cupped her buttocks and pulled her tight into him. He moved his hips, nudged her legs apart and inserted one of his own. The proof of his desire lay hot and hard along her thigh, and her woman's center responded.

She melted inside for him, wanted nothing more than to make love with him.…

Except to get Lester and his accomplice safely under lock and key.

Ignoring the throbbing between her thighs, she tore her mouth free and pushed at Lucky's chest. He loosened his hold but didn't let go.

"We don't have time to get carried away," she whispered, breathing hard.

His gaze seared her face. "You're right. This isn't the time."

Meaning there would be another time? she wondered hopefully.

"We have plans to make," she said. "A trap to set."

"I still don't like using you as the cheese…but I can tell you're determined."

"I don't see any other way."

With a sigh, Lucky nodded and let go of her. JoJo immediately felt the loss but kept her melancholy to herself. Once danger had been defeated, they would have time to satisfy their passion for one another. Beyond that, JoJo wasn't willing to imagine, no matter her crazy feelings.

She might be falling hard for Lucky Donatelli, but she wasn't going to count on anything, especially not a future that included him.

The sun was in the process of setting by the time everyone but Caroline had gathered around the fireplace. JoJo had noticed her car was gone when she'd returned to the main house. There was still no sign of Lucky's sister.

"So what should we do tonight?" Paula asked. "Other than pick a new restaurant for dinner, that is? I know—a place that has country dancing would be fun."

"Not for me," JoJo announced. "I'm going to raid the fridge and spend a nice quiet night here. *Alone,*" she emphasized.

"Eli and I have plans," Lucky said.

"Me, too." Adair stood before the fireplace. "I'm meeting one of the other stuntmen from *Call of the West* for dinner. But thanks for the invite."

"I guess it's just you and me," Rocky said, giving Paula a meaningful look.

Paula smiled and hooked a hunk of hair behind her ear. "Right. I'll figure out something to keep us entertained."

JoJo was certain she would.

Dusk was deepening over the land by the time everyone filed out. She was relieved that everything was going according to plan—her alone and everyone knowing it. Then Lester was sure to know it, as well. Being the bait in this game of cat and mouse was a little nerve-wracking, but she was committed to trapping Lester. It wouldn't be long now. She began turning on lights to make certain he'd be able to see her clearly through the windows when he arrived.

The telephone ringing made her start. Wondering if this could be Lucky, JoJo crossed the room, eager to hear his voice if not his reassurances. But when she picked up the receiver, she was surprised to find another Donatelli on the line.

"JoJo, that you?"

"Sally? Uh, Caroline's not here at the moment," JoJo said, wondering if he knew about Lucky's appearance. "I can take a message—"

"No message. I wanna talk to *you.*"

"Me?"

"I hear you had some trouble the last coupla days." Caroline must be keeping him well informed. "Nothing fatal."

"Don't joke. Death isn't funny, but it's permanent. I been worried about you."

"I appreciate your concern, Sally." JoJo figured she might as well bring him up to date. "And I have at least some idea of what's been going on. When Caroline told me about Lester Perkins, I should have—"

"I told her to say nothing!"

"It's a good thing she did, or I'd have thought I was crazy this afternoon. Lester's here, in Sedona."

"Crissakes! How'd he figure out where you were?"

"He had help." And maybe Sally could tell her from whom. "Did Lester have family—a brother or a cousin—or some close friend that you know of?"

"His mama died about a dozen years back, and he didn't have no sisters or brothers. I couldn't say about a cousin. As for a friend . . . you know Lester was peculiar."

"I know." But why would some stranger help Lester escape from the psych ward?

"Maybe you better come back to Las Vegas right away," Sally suggested.

"I can't. We, uh, I have a plan."

JoJo grimaced. She'd almost slipped and told him about Lucky. She figured if Sally knew his son was around, he would have mentioned him. JoJo certainly didn't want to be the one to let the cat out of the bag—Lucky would hold that against her, she was sure. Still, it was pretty odd that Sally *didn't* seem to know.

Was Caroline's loyalty to her brother stronger than that to her father? Or was Lucky's sister holding out because of some other motive?

"I can guard you better here."

Wondering if he was as protective of all Nick's friends, JoJo said, "Don't worry about it, Sally. I'm not coming back to Las Vegas until I have him where I want him."

An unexpected sound behind JoJo prompted her to whirl around only to face Lucky, who stood in the doorway. Her throat tightened. From his sour expression, she knew he'd heard what she'd just told his father—and she expected he was thinking the worst.

She didn't take her eyes off the son when she told the father, "Listen, I have to go now."

"JoJo, wait a minute—" Sally was saying even as she dropped the phone into its cradle.

"I didn't expect you to come back."

"How surprising," he said dryly. "Did you have enough time to give my father a full update?"

JoJo tried to be straight with him. "Sally called me because he'd heard about the accidents. That's it. He was concerned."

"And you reassured him that you were still in one piece ... as you were reassuring him about your plans concerning me when I walked in."

He really did think the worst of her. He wasn't even willing to ask her for her side of the story before making accusations.

Disappointed but not surprised, she said, "So you assume."

"If you weren't talking about me, then who?"

"You're so smart, you figure it out!"

They glared at each other. Stalemate. He wasn't backing down. And neither was she.

Finally, Lucky broke the silence. "Zamora came in from the range with three Macbride wranglers. They've been briefed and are ready."

A thrill of nerves shot through JoJo, and she was hard-pressed to keep her voice from being sharp. "You're sure Lester won't spot them?"

"I'm not sure of anything," Lucky admitted, and JoJo knew he wasn't merely talking about the situation with Lester. He indicated the battery-operated lantern he'd been holding. "Use this when you leave the house." He set it next to the door. "I'd better get going."

"I guess you'd better."

No soft words. No kindness in his eyes. He might as well be a stranger. Heartsick that he was being such a damn fool—that she was such a damn fool for caring what he thought of her—JoJo was glad to see the last of Lucky for the moment. Later, she would vent her feelings, but for now she needed to keep her wits about her.

Taking a couple of apples from a hanging wire holder, she chopped them into chunks and threw the pieces into a plastic bag that she left on the counter.

Night had fallen, an inky darkness spreading beyond the windows. She could no longer see out except for the lighted driveway, but anyone outside could see in.

Doing normal things—pouring a soda, fluffing a pillow on the couch before making herself comfortable, browsing through a magazine—was more difficult than she might have imagined. With each minute

that passed, the temptation to stare at the windows
and search for a reflection or some small movement
grew stronger.

"Come on, Lester," she muttered under her breath.
"Cooperate for once. Let us take you in. Don't make
anyone hurt you."

She shouldn't be worried about the former maintenance man. He'd tracked her down, after all, obviously to get revenge. He was willing to hurt her, if not
worse. Right? But Lester wasn't playing with a full
deck, she reminded herself, and not so long ago his
intentions toward her were good. He'd tried to protect her. He'd stopped her from making the biggest
mistake of her life.

She owed him this.

The seconds ticked away. JoJo kept up the pretense
of reading when her mind was everywhere but on the
magazine. Finally, when she thought she could stand
waiting no longer, the clock above the fireplace indicated more than an hour had passed. It was time.

Keeping her movements casual, she rose and
stretched, first her shoulders, then the small of her
back, finally her legs. Time to take a little walk. She
made a trip to the counter, where she retrieved the bag
of apple slices and stuffed it in a vest pocket.

Anticipation washed over her as she casually approached the front entrance. *He* could be on the other
side. Lester. Her hand hovered over the knob. Once
she opened the door, he could shove her back in, and
before anyone could come to her rescue, he could do
unspeakable things to her.

He could kill her.

And yet, she had no sense of Lester's presence.

JoJo was counting on there being no surprise attack, on Lester's waiting out there at some distance, on his following her wherever she would lead him. She was counting on his wanting a verbal confrontation with her before he did anything else. Face-to-face. He'd done as much for Mia Scudella.

And Mia Scudella had died at his hands, she reminded herself.

She wouldn't let her guard down for a moment.

Her fingers curled around the knob and turned it. The door swung open. A gust of wind chilled her, and she thought to fetch a sweater.

A delaying tactic.

Recognizing the instinct, she instead grabbed the lantern Lucky had brought her and stepped out into the night.

Every nerve humming, she switched on the power, the glowing gold light turning her into a moving target as she sauntered toward the outbuildings and the horse pasture. The idea of the plan was to draw Lester out into the open, where Lucky and the men could get to him. She'd barely gotten a quarter of the way to the pasture when she felt it—the fine hairs on the back of her neck standing up.

Instinct warned her of a malevolent presence.

Her breath thickened. Her pulse raced. She wanted to run like hell.

Somehow, she kept walking. Slowly. Steadily. As if she hadn't a care in the world. Lester was out there in the dark somewhere.

Watching her.

As were another half-dozen sets of eyes, she reminded herself. She was going to be all right.

JoJo kept moving, kept facing forward, but her gaze strayed from side to side. In vain, of course. She couldn't even discern where Lucky and his men lay in wait. Her mouth went dry, and her heartbeat thundered through her ears against the whinny of a horse, followed by a snort from the nearby enclosure, telling her that Bushwhacker was not yet asleep.

A single light softly illuminated the area in front of the small pasture where the riding horses grazed. Her goal. When she got to the split-rail fence, she turned off the lantern and set it on the ground. Then she pursed her lips and whistled sharply several times, her radar attuned to the area behind and to her sides.

"Spitfire!" she called, pulling the bag of apple pieces from her pocket. "Here, girl."

Snorts and the *clop-clop* of hoofed feet told her more than one horse was wandering her way. No sound made by a human alerted her.

"Spitfire, look what I have for you," she crooned, sticking her hand through the split rails.

The little mare sped up, eager for the treat. Her soft lips culled the apple from JoJo's palm. She dipped into the plastic bag as Silverado pushed his head toward her to investigate. Then another horse crowded the first two.

If she weren't so on edge, JoJo thought, she would be enjoying the animals' attention. As it was, she had to restrain herself from dumping the contents of the bag and heading back to the ranch house as fast as her legs would carry her. Getting more and more tense as she waited for Lester to make his move, she forced herself to divvy up the apple pieces, one at a time. But the bag emptied and he still hadn't shown.

What to do?

She stalled, heart in her throat, fussing over the horses for as long as she could interest them. But when they fathomed she had no more treats, fickle creatures that they were, the animals wandered off in search of sweet grass, literally leaving JoJo holding the bag.

Damn you, Lester, make your move! she thought.

Nothing.

Stuffing the plastic in her vest pocket, she picked up the lantern and played with it for a moment, as if it weren't working properly.

Still no movement. No sound.

Not knowing what else to do, JoJo switched on the light and set off. Disappointment washed through her. She'd been so certain he was out there, so certain this plan would work. He'd forced her hand. She'd have to call the authorities. She couldn't go on like this.

The moment she let her guard down, a noise to her left made her miss a step. Stumbling, she dropped the lantern and whirled around crazily. In the middle of the outbuilding yard, JoJo came face-to-face with the man she now feared. The man she had once liked. The man she still felt sorry for. Golden light from the lantern on the ground washed up and over him, making him look damn spooky.

"Lester," she said far more calmly than she was feeling. Her heart seemed both to be dashing itself against her ribs and climbing into her throat.

"JoJo, I knew I'd find you." Lester punched at his glasses and, eyes wide behind the thick lenses, peered around. "It's not safe here. We have to go."

JoJo forced herself to stare straight at him rather than look around for Lucky and the others and chance warning him. "Why do you want to hurt me, Lester?"

"C'mon, JoJo." Before she could back away, he grabbed her arm, his grip steely. "We have to go," he repeated, this time with a sense of urgency that transferred itself to her.

Still, she fought him, but the more JoJo struggled, the more determined Lester seemed to drag her off into the dark. She dug her heels and her weight into the earth, but that only slowed him down some.

Where the hell was Lucky?

"Let her go, Lester!" came a male shout, but the voice wasn't the one she expected to hear.

"No, you'll hurt her."

"You're the one hurting her," Adair said agreeably.

JoJo got a glimpse of the gun in his hand—he was aiming it straight at them.

A shot rang out and Adair whipped around, blindly pointing in the right direction and pulling the trigger. A loud click echoed across the yard. JoJo gasped—he'd never realized she'd emptied his clip. Despite the weapon in his hand, he was unarmed. A repeat shot from the dark and Adair jerked back, the gun flying from his hand.

A frantic Lester was dragging a still-struggling JoJo from the center of the yard inches at a time.

"Go! Get her out of here!" Adair shouted at Lester, even as another bullet drove into him.

He seemed to explode forward before toppling, face to the ground.

Suddenly armed men were appearing from every direction. Lucky was the first to get to her and her would-be captor. Lester was sobbing and jerking at

JoJo's arm ineffectually. She was so stunned by what had happened to Adair Keating that she stood frozen, staring at his body. She'd been right about the supposed stuntman, after all.

"Let her go now, Lester," Lucky said calmly. "You remember me, right?" He took off his hat so the other man could see his face more clearly in the dim yard light.

"Mr. D's...brother...Lucky," Lester said between sobs.

"You trust me, don't you, Lester?"

"I don't know," he keened, rocking on his heels. "I don't know. I don't know."

"I don't want to hurt you. Or JoJo. You don't want to see JoJo hurt, either, right?"

"No. Don't hurt JoJo."

"Then let her go." Lucky reached out and got a firm grip on the man even as Lester released her arm.

"She's okay now," Lester said, talking more to himself than to them. "JoJo's okay."

"This guy ain't." Eli was bending over Adair, turning him over and feeling for a pulse. "He's still alive. Somebody call for an ambulance."

As JoJo forced her feet to move, one after the other, until she was standing over Adair, Lucky dispatched a wrangler named Bubba to make the call, adding that he should get someone from the sheriff's office over to the ranch, as well. Then he assigned two other men to guard Lester.

"Don't turn your back on him," he warned them. "He's slippery when he wants to be."

JoJo heard it all as if from a distance. She'd been correct about Adair. If she hadn't lifted the bullets, he might have shot someone. Like her.

But why?

She glanced over at Lester, whose thin arms were wrapped around his bony frame. He was shuddering, and his lips were moving as if he were mumbling to himself. She doubted he could answer any straight questions at the moment.

Like why he would stalk her...then say he didn't want her hurt.

JoJo shook her head. Lester was confused. Suggestible. That was no surprise. They might never get the truth out of him. Or out of Adair, if he didn't survive. Eli had stripped off his shirt and was pressing it to Adair's chest wound, trying to stop the bleeding.

Suddenly JoJo realized she was shaking and her stomach was turning over. She ran for the bushes and was thankful the men gave her some privacy while she was sick.

"When the sheriff's men get here," she heard Lucky say, "they'll want a complete report. So who shot Adair?"

One of the men guarding Lester spoke up. "Not me."

"I never fired my rifle," claimed the other.

"Me, neither," Vincent added.

"Don't look at me," Eli groused as he shifted his weight over Adair's chest wound. "You know how I feel about guns. Wouldn't touch one if it up and bit me."

"Must have been Bubba, then," Lucky said.

But when Bubba returned a few minutes later, having made both phone calls as instructed, he denied having used his weapon, as well.

"The man's lying there bleeding to death!" Lucky shouted. "Someone damn well shot him!"

Her stomach emptied, JoJo drew closer to him and caught his gaze. They stared at each other, the question stretching between them—if none of the men guarding her had shot Adair, then who had?

Chapter Twelve

The identity of the man who'd shot Adair was still plaguing JoJo early the next morning. If one of the men had lied, her best guess would be Vincent. Unfortunately, no one had checked all the guns to make certain the men were telling the truth. She was wondering what Lucky's take on the situation was when he drove up to the ranch house a little past dawn. JoJo wondered if he'd been out all night, or if he'd bunked over at the Wrangler's Roost for some reason.

Though she was still too upset to be hungry, she was setting the table for breakfast when she heard his key in the door. Everyone would have to eat, including her.

Quietly entering the house, Lucky seemed surprised. "You're up early."

How personal. What did she expect? That he'd take her in his arms and ask if she was okay? He hadn't even done that the night before—and after she'd been sick. She wondered how much more sentiment he would have shown if Adair had actually shot her.

Probably wouldn't have made a bit of difference, she thought sadly.

"I didn't sleep too well," JoJo told him, her voice stiff. "Nightmares kept waking me all night, so I figured I might as well get up and do something useful." Her hand filled with flatware, she hung on tight and took a big breath. "Have you had any news?"

"Adair came through surgery all right. The doctors say he's stable, but he's still unconscious."

She received the announcement dispassionately. "What about Lester?" When she'd left the sheriff's office late the night before, he'd still been crying and babbling to himself, unable or unwilling to give any explanations.

"No change. No matter what anyone asked him about his escape or how he got to Sedona or why he wanted to hurt you, he just kept repeating, 'JoJo's safe now,' or something to that effect." Lucky shook his head in bafflement. "And we still have no idea of who shot Adair."

A fact that bothered her. "Do you think one of the men was lying?"

"To protect himself? Maybe. I wish the deputy sheriff had thought to check their weapons to see if they'd been fired."

"You thought of it."

"My asking would've been an insult. I'll be working with these men. I need their trust."

Something he didn't seem too willing to give a person, JoJo thought. "Yeah, that's more important than finding out who shot a man and why." She was glad when Lucky shifted and looked discomfited. "I guess we'll have to wait till Adair comes around to get a clue." She continued setting the flatware next to the plates.

Lucky was silent for a moment. Then, his tone hollow, he said, "I don't think you should wait. I think you should get back to Las Vegas. This morning, if at all possible."

She stared at him, at the face that she knew almost as well as she knew her own—broken nose, scarred chin and forehead, broad mouth pulled into a straight line, pale eyes flat. She'd come to like that face and love the man wearing it, but he obviously had no such feelings for her.

JoJo swallowed her hurt. "Yeah, maybe I *should* leave." Eyes stinging, she threw down the rest of the flatware and rushed past him, determined that he wouldn't see her cry.

"JoJo—"

Pausing, she kept her back to him. "What?"

"Never mind."

JoJo continued into her room and dug out her suitcases. Damn Lucky Donatelli! Couldn't he even pretend he cared, just a little? Or was he so obsessed with his love-hate relationship with his father that he didn't have room for other people, other emotions?

She almost wished that Sally hadn't called the night before . . . and yet, if Lucky was so bent on believing she was working for his father despite her telling him differently numerous times, better that she know it now.

She packed with a vengeance, and only while stuffing a magazine back into the zippered compartment of her large suitcase did she remember the letter from the New York law office that she'd left half-read. She'd promised herself to get back to it for days, and now was as good a time as any. Finding the missive, she sat on the edge of the bed and pulled the letter from its envelope.

Dear Miss Weston:
With regret we must inform you of the passing of Oliver Phipps. On the morning of June 3, he had a massive heart attack and never recovered.

Mr. Phipps regarded you highly and wanted to ensure a comfortable future for you. To that end, he made a generous provision for you in his will.

Please contact our office as soon as possible so we can make the necessary arrangements to carry out Oliver's last wishes.

Sincerely,
Kenneth Abrams

JoJo broke down and cried. Oliver had left her some money, bless his heart. She knew he'd meant to leave his estate to various charities and foundations since he had no immediate family, but he'd included her. He'd always said he meant to take care of her, and he'd done so even though she'd left New York and him.

At least Oliver had cherished her. Totally unlike Lucky.

Pushing thoughts of the unfeeling man from her mind, JoJo considered what "generous provision" meant—that she wouldn't have to worry about growing too old to be a show girl? She could probably start that small business any time she wanted. If she could figure out what she was interested in doing and where she wanted to live, that was.

JoJo dried her eyes, blew her nose and finished packing. Then she went through her closet and drawers one last time to make certain she hadn't forgotten anything . . . and was suddenly reminded of the Soleri bell and the postcards she'd bought at Tlaquepaque. She hadn't packed them, so where in the heck were they?

It took a moment to realize she'd left them in Paula's car. On the chance that the vehicle had been left open, JoJo went to investigate. Flora was in the kitchen area, starting breakfast, but stopped what she was doing the moment she saw JoJo.

"I heard what happened last night." The housekeeper sounded concerned. "You are all right?"

"I'm fine," JoJo lied. She was alive and unscathed on the outside. But inside was another story. She knew such a thing wasn't really possible, but her heart felt as if it were ready to break. "I'm preparing to leave, actually. Probably after breakfast."

Flora nodded. "Perhaps this is best."

Perhaps it was. No point in staying around, mooning over Lucky. The sooner she left, the sooner she could start getting over him. To that end, she continued on her mission to recover her purchases, trying not to worry that getting over Lucky might prove impossible. She hadn't felt half as devastated when Mac had become Marco and she'd learned he was a murderer!

As she'd hoped, Paula hadn't locked the rental car. But when JoJo opened the rear door, the back seat was clear. Her package had slid to the floor. Retrieving the bag, she heard a plastic rattle—the object that had dropped from the CD case when she'd picked it up the day before. An empty audiotape box. She returned it to the leather tote and went back into the house.

A few minutes later, her things in order, JoJo was physically if not psychologically ready to leave for Las Vegas. She planned to get on the road after getting something to eat. Breakfast smells invaded her bedroom, enticing her. She was hungry, after all.

Paula, Rocky and Caroline were already at the table, and Flora was setting down platters of sausage and pancakes. JoJo wondered if Lucky or Eli intended to show for breakfast. Part of her hoped not—undoubtedly, leaving without seeing Lucky again would be easier.

"Still in one piece," Caroline drawled, her green gaze mocking. "I did warn you about Lester."

She had at that, JoJo thought. "I guess I should thank you."

"Don't strain yourself."

"Why didn't you tell us what was going on yesterday?" Paula demanded.

And Rocky complained, "We got back from town after the excitement was all over. Vincent filled us in."

Though JoJo wondered when Caroline had arrived, she didn't ask. Undoubtedly, Vincent had filled her in, as well. Either the wrangler or Lucky.

To JoJo's disappointment, Lucky never made an appearance at the breakfast table. That she might have seen the last of him hit her, and her appetite waned quickly.

Near the end of the meal, Paula asked, "How about we take another ride this morning, JoJo?"

"I'm going back to Las Vegas."

The other woman looked shocked. "You're kidding! Today?"

"In a few minutes."

"Oh, come on. You don't really have to leave so early, do you? I mean, you don't have an appointment or someone waiting for you?"

"Well, no, but—"

"I didn't think so. You can spare another couple of hours for a friend. Even if you leave here early this afternoon, you should be able to get back to Las Vegas before dark. Pretty please?" Paula gave her a pleading expression. "After what's been happening around here over the past few days, I don't feel comfortable riding alone."

Not wanting to be swayed, JoJo said, "Rocky would be better protection."

"Uh, you gotta be kidding." He laughed. "I got saddle sores from the other day."

When JoJo glanced at Caroline, Lucky's sister merely arched her eyebrows in a don't-even-ask expression.

JoJo sighed. "All right. A short ride."

"Great!"

A delaying tactic in hopes that she would catch sight of Lucky, JoJo realized. For once she left the ranch, she would probably never see him again.

"So, YOU FIGURED what this mess was about?" Eli asked Lucky as they sprawled in the living area of the Wrangler's Roost and downed stale coffee.

"Beats me." Lucky set down his mug and began checking over his lariat for any frays or weak spots. "Lester Perkins might have tracked JoJo to Sedona somehow, but I'd bet my last buck he didn't mean her any harm."

"Someone did. Adair Keating?"

"If so, JoJo couldn't say."

Lucky considered the slight possibility that Keating and Lester were related or old friends, and that Keating had been trying to get revenge for Lester . . . but he didn't buy it. He could hardly believe his gut instincts about JoJo's working for his father had been wrong. Still, he knew something more than met the eye was going on here, and that JoJo would be safer in Las Vegas until they could get to the bottom of this.

Envisioning JoJo's expression when he'd suggested she leave again made Lucky squirm in his chair. She hadn't been able to hide her hurt. Hurt suggested caring. Well . . . back at her. He had more feelings for the redhead than he knew what to do with.

Despite his suspicions and determination to keep her at arm's length emotionally if not physically, JoJo had earned his grudging respect and trust. His doubts had sprouted like devil's horns, however, when he'd interrupted her phone conversation with his father. But maybe he'd purposely misunderstood because he'd wanted an out.

When all was said and done, though, the thought of JoJo's leaving—of the likelihood of his not seeing her again—left Lucky empty inside.

Question was—what was he willing to do about her?

"Think Keating'll ever open his eyes and talk?" Eli was asking.

The question brought Lucky back to the conversation at hand. "Maybe he already has. I oughta call to check." Staring at the lariat in his hands, he thought to trade the rope for the telephone when a loud drone outside snapped him to attention. "What the hell's that?"

Eli sprang to his feet. "Sounds like a whirlybird!"

"Sounds like trouble to me."

Throwing the looped lariat around his shoulder, Lucky grabbed a rifle from the gun rack and checked to make certain it was loaded, then stuffed some additional ammunition in a vest pocket.

"Let's go meet trouble head-on," Lucky said grimly.

The men exited in time to see a chopper descending near the main house. Gripping the rifle, Lucky took off through the wooded area, Eli on his heels. By the time he broke through the growth, the chopper had touched down and Caroline was at the opening.

Lucky didn't have to see him to know the identity of the main passenger.

Vito Tolentino alighted first, looked around to make certain all was clear, then gave the man inside the high sign. Lucky slowed down, but kept walking. No matter what JoJo thought, he wasn't afraid. Besides, a confrontation was inevitable. He might as well get it over with.

"That who I think it is?" Eli puffed from directly behind him.

"Yeah. Salvatore Donatelli—the great man himself has come to call."

He watched his father debark and hug his sister.

"Papa, I've missed you," Caroline shouted above the beating sound of the chopper's blades.

"You wanna tell me what in bloody hell is going on around here?"

Feet rooted to the earth, Lucky took a good look at the man he hadn't seen in person since he was a kid. Sally Donatelli was an older version of his firstborn. He was a little stockier than Nick, his face a bit more jowly, but the resemblance was unmistakable.

Suddenly, as if he *knew,* Sally looked past his daughter. His smile slowly faded. "Lucky."

His father didn't look any happier than he was feeling, Lucky realized. Clenching the rifle tightly, Lucky stepped forward as his father and sister stepped from beneath the whirling blades. He was short of arm's reach of the older man.

"What are you doing here?" he demanded over the noise of the chopper.

"That any way to greet your father?"

"You didn't answer my question."

Sally sighed. "Sometimes a man's gotta handle things himself."

Lucky tightened his jaw. So it was to begin. "You mean about bringing me home?"

"I mean about keeping JoJo safe. How Adair Keating got himself shot, I don't understand."

Not expecting this, Lucky was nonplussed. "*You* don't understand? What's Keating to you?"

"He works for me. When I heard Lester Perkins escaped, I sent him here to keep an eye on JoJo."

So Adair Keating hadn't sprung Lester...nor had he been the one to create those accidents for JoJo. His gut instincts had proved correct once more.

"Keating didn't do a very good job," Lucky said dryly. And damn him, he couldn't help himself. "And you could have called JoJo back to Vegas," he tested, just to be certain.

His father's expression was perplexed. "What makes you think JoJo would do anything *I* said?"

"Then she's not working for you?" Lucky asked, to be perfectly clear.

"Whatever gave you such an idea? She's a good kid. A friend of Nick's. You remember him—your brother?" Sally said sarcastically.

Just as she'd told him over and over. Just as he'd been beginning to believe.

Lucky didn't react, merely asked, "If she's not yours, then why did you send someone to look after her?"

"Old Lester went off the beam and gave her a damn hard time a coupla months back. He's my responsibility—I promised his mama I'd take care of him before she died. After what he put JoJo through, she deserves some peace. Plus, she's got guts and I admire her." His father glared at him. "That good enough for you, smart boy?"

The explanation should have been good enough when JoJo had given it to him the first time, Lucky realized. Guilt swamped him. Despite all her denials, he'd held her accountable, and though deep inside, he'd slowly come to believe he was wrong, he'd never put words to his change of heart. He'd never told *her*. Now JoJo would never consider that he'd come to trust her on his own, and somehow, Lucky knew how important that would be to her.

"JoJo thought Keating was the one who helped Lester escape," Lucky finally said. "If he wasn't the one . . ."

"It has to be someone else around here," Eli finished.

"Oh, my God," Caroline murmured, looking truly concerned. "Rocky did a disappearing act right after JoJo agreed to go out riding with Paula."

Opening herself to new dangers, Lucky realized, heart in his throat. He concluded his own question: if Keating wasn't guilty, then Rocky had to be.

"I'm going after her." Hoping he wasn't too late to stop Rocky Franzone from whatever devious plan he had in mind, Lucky started for the pasture and Silverado.

"Lucky, wait!" Caroline said, stopping him. "If JoJo's in danger now, you'll never get to her in time on a horse!"

Lucky whipped around. "What do you suggest?"

And knew he was staring at the answer.

"I'M GOING TO MISS this country," JoJo said sincerely as she and Paula picked their way through a small, creek-fed canyon.

The setting was beautiful. Tall ponderosa pines were dwarfed by sheer erosion-carved walls. And though the sun's rays had difficulty penetrating this part of the deep, narrow gorge, walnut and maple trees lined the creek's bank in addition to the conifers.

"It's not like you live so far that you can't come back any time you want," Paula said.

"If I had a reason."

"What? Lucky's not enough reason for you?"

As usual, Paula was man-obsessed, as if a relationship were the key to solving any problem. Well, this time, she had a point, JoJo admitted. Lucky *was* the problem.

"He's enough," JoJo admitted, guiding Spitfire around some boulders strewn across the rough path and through the water. "It's just—"

"That he's not flush?" Paula finished for her.

"I don't care about money."

Paula snorted. "*Everyone* cares about money. But you don't really have to worry about it, do you?"

The comment struck JoJo wrong somehow. Made her uneasy. She'd known all along that Paula was one for creature comforts that far exceeded what she could afford on a secretary's salary—her English-riding training, the jewelry she coveted, the need for an expensive rental car.

Thinking about the car triggered a new, elusive unease.

That Paula was indicating *she* was somehow better off irritated JoJo. "Being a show girl has its rewards, but not many of us get rich off the profession."

"I wasn't thinking about your salary."

Reminded of her recent windfall that *would* make those things affordable soon, JoJo frowned and scrutinized the other woman, but Paula's expression was placid. She couldn't possibly know. JoJo didn't get it . . . unless Paula was a snoop and had gone through her things . . . and so had found the letter from the lawyers.

Taking a guess at the other's woman problem, she asked, "Did your ex-husband leave you with big debts or something?"

When Paula admitted "There is no ex-husband," JoJo started.

"So you didn't come to the ranch to mend a broken heart?"

"That part is true. I just wasn't married like I thought I would be when it was time to say goodbye."

Paula sounded regretful, as if she'd rather be divorced than just left by a lover, JoJo thought, unable to figure out why the other woman had lied about her situation.

"You didn't have to keep the nature of your relationship a secret. Just because you weren't married doesn't make a breakup any less painful."

As JoJo herself was full aware. Lucky would haunt her. She'd see that devilish grin of his until the day she died.

"I don't like having to explain myself. Not usually. But I'll make this an exception," Paula said with a smile that looked a bit forced. "Why don't we get down, stretch our legs and give our butts a rest, and I'll tell you all about it."

"Sure," JoJo agreed, though she suddenly felt edgy. "Then we'd better turn back. I need to get on the road if I don't want to be driving through the desert in the dark."

They dismounted. Salmon sandstone walls closed in around them, creating a shelter of murky shadows and fragile breezes. While the place could be a private haven, at the moment it had the opposite effect on JoJo. A little spooked by the isolation, she was glad when Paula led her horse a bit farther to an open area splashed with sunshine and a leg of the creek. They were watering their horses when an odd sound reverberated along the canyon walls.

"What's that?" JoJo asked, shading her eyes as she looked up.

The sound grew louder, hurting her ears and agitating the horses, as a helicopter swept by overhead. JoJo hung on to Spitfire and soothed the mare with low tones.

"Tourists," Paula stated, rubbing her horse's neck. And when the helicopter vanished and the sound faded off, she said, "You have to understand my background, JoJo. I grew up with money. My family had everything. An estate. Cars. Horses. The best education."

"Why am I not surprised?"

JoJo had guessed Paula wasn't exactly what she'd seemed, though she'd figured it had been a successful husband who'd gotten her used to luxury.

"My father foolishly made some bad investments. A multitude of bad investments. He lost everything when I was twenty. Then he killed himself." In a strange little voice, she added, "Without money, what hope did I have of finding a good catch? I couldn't even finish my degree in music."

Music…the CDs…and a lone audiotape box…

Pulse thrumming, JoJo said, "So your life changed."

"Drastically. I was on my own, and things were tough for years. Then I met this wonderful man right after Thanksgiving. I was playing the piano at a society party, and he couldn't resist. He was older, sophisticated, perfect for me. Everything I'd ever dreamed of in a potential husband. We had similar backgrounds and interests and got along famously. On Christmas Eve, he asked me to move in with him. By New Year's Eve, we were living together. But every day I spent with him I knew part of him longed for another woman. I tried to make him happy. I swore he was."

JoJo's pulse surged. She had an awful feeling….
"He broke up with you?"

"Actually, he died."

"It's terrible to lose someone you love." Suspecting she knew what was coming, JoJo choked the words out. "What happened? An accident?"

"A heart attack," Paula said. "And losing him *was* awful, but what came after was even worse."

Part of JoJo was thinking about the significance of an empty audiotape box in a car that had only a CD player. Part of her was saying, "I don't understand."

And when Paula stated "It was the will," JoJo's heart sank. "I knew he'd earmarked most of his estate to charitable organizations and foundations, but I figured he would leave me—the woman who'd shared the last five months of his life—well, at least a little something. I was wrong. It was *you* he honored in his will."

JoJo whispered, "Oliver Phipps."

"*I* was Oliver's companion when he died. *I* deserved to be remembered. It isn't fair. I've talked to the best lawyers in New York. They tell me that since we weren't married, I can't possibly contest the philanthropic bequests that were set up years ago. But as his recognized companion, I can contest the codicil—the money he left you. And if something should happen to you, the process would be that much easier, the outcome that much more certain."

"So it's been you all along." Not Lester. Not Adair. JoJo was numb with shock. "*You've* been trying to kill me."

"I'm sorry, JoJo. You're a nice person. I like you. I like you a lot."

The whirling drone returned, and above them, the helicopter glided by in the opposite direction.

JoJo hung on to her nervous horse. Her thoughts were whirling, trying to make connections. "Lester... you broke him out?"

"With help."

"Why?" she asked, wondering who had helped Paula with her evil plan.

"Insurance, of course. If I had to resort to drastic measures, I counted on him being the patsy. I kept a tab on you all along, JoJo. I wanted to know my competition. Using Lester was a natural. I followed you from Vegas, had Rocky set Lester up in a cheap motel while I made my entrance at the ranch. Lester was so grateful that we needed his help. I convinced him I was your friend and that you were in trouble again. When I left you at Tlaquepaque to make that phone call, it was so Rocky could get Lester close enough for you to see. So you could name him. He's still in love with you—as deluded by the unavailable as Oliver was."

"I never lied to Oliver," JoJo insisted, the numbness wearing off, the fear making her wary. What was Paula up to? "I didn't try to trick him."

"Remember what we talked about over lunch— about us girls having to take care of ourselves? That's all I'm doing. I'm sure you understand I have to take care of myself just like you did when you used your wiles on Oliver so that he would include you in his will."

"But I never—"

"Don't try to deny it!"

JoJo's mouth snapped shut when Paula stepped from behind her horse, a gun in her hand.

Chapter Thirteen

"Bring me back over that canyon!" Lucky yelled at the chopper pilot.

"Yes, sir!"

Certain he'd seen a vehicle half-hidden by trees at the top of the plateau, Lucky leaned out of the opening slightly. As the chopper circled, he got a better view of the area through a set of binoculars. Sure enough, there it was—JoJo's red Cherokee. And only one person could have driven the Jeep out here. A second later, Lucky spotted the bastard and drew back slightly so he couldn't be seen himself.

Flat against the cliff's top, Rocky Franzone lay waiting to ambush JoJo. For a second, he glanced up at the chopper, then, obviously unsuspecting, went back to the sight of his high-powered rifle.

Not about to lose the woman he loved, Lucky was tempted to shoot Rocky where he lay. But if he did, he'd probably kill the criminal. They might never learn why he was after JoJo—or if others were involved.

Lucky couldn't take that chance.

As they flew along the gorge, Lucky could see straight to the bottom. JoJo was already there with Paula, both women on foot near the creek, hanging on to their horses, who danced and threw up their heads from the noise. With no time to lose, he issued new orders to the pilot.

Again, the chopper made a wide arc and swept toward the ambush site, descending as swiftly as was safe. Lodged in the opening behind the pilot, Lucky grabbed his lariat, fastened one end to the aircraft and hung on tight.

He had a clear view of Rocky, who was shouldering the rifle and taking aim. The noise of the blades broke the concentration of the would-be assassin. Rocky glanced up again. Face reflecting his alarm at the aircraft's third approach, he rolled to his back, taking the rifle with him.

Only yards away, Lucky gave the command, "Now!" and leaned out of the opening as the man on the ground bounced to his feet.

The chopper hovered in one spot, and the lariat whirled in a widening loop before Rocky could hike the rifle to his shoulder and take aim. Lucky released and the loop went sailing over the man's head and shoulders. As Lucky quickly tightened the leather around his arms and chest, Rocky was still fumbling with the rifle ineffectually.

"Lift!" Lucky yelled, and a shot went wild.

The chopper rose several yards nearly straight up, Rocky coming with it. The rope tightened around his chest, below his shoulders, but he panicked and let go of the weapon to find a handhold anyway. The rifle bounced against his flailing legs…then dropped to the ground with a thunk.

THE COMBINED SOUND of helicopter and rifle shot sent a quiver along Spitfire's flesh. The high-strung horse threw up her head and screamed in fear... and JoJo let go of the reins, urging the mare toward Paula as a diversion. Spitfire nearly ran her down, creating an effective block between the two women for a few moments.

The chance JoJo needed.

She didn't think, but acted on sheer instinct, running for all she was worth.

With Paula's screech of frustration ringing in her ears—and the splash of the gun going into the drink, to boot—JoJo searched wildly for a place to hide. It wouldn't take the other woman long to retrieve the weapon and be after her. JoJo didn't fool herself that the gun wouldn't fire just because it was a little wet.

Above, the helicopter hovered. Not slowing, JoJo gave it a quick glance and swore she saw a body dancing from the end of a rope.

Ahead, she couldn't miss the narrowing walls of the canyon. The red cliffs loomed barely more than a few yards apart.

Below, the stream was choked with rocks and boulders at its edges and formed a long, shadowed pool that looked too deep to cross, while the path simply disappeared.

Behind, she heard Paula coming after her.

JoJo's heart flailed itself against her ribs as she tried to make up her mind.

What to do?

LUCKY BARELY HEARD Rocky's "Let me down, you son of a bitch, before you hang me!" over the ear-splitting noise of the whirling blades above.

"I'd like to let you down, all right," Lucky muttered, "straight into a stand of cactus."

No chance the man would actually hang—unless he managed to work the rope above his shoulders. He damn well might do it, too! Lucky feared.

The pilot yelled, "What now?"

"Set us down!" Lucky returned. "And be careful you don't squash the bastard like the cockroach he is!"

They slowly descended, the pilot maneuvering the craft away from the spot where Rocky landed. The man's legs collapsed under him, and he fell to his knees. But he was a tough bastard, up on his feet and working at the rope even as Lucky hurled himself out of the chopper.

Rocky went down again, this time with Lucky on top of him. The men rolled away from the aircraft toward the edge of the cliff, the loose rope tangling around them. Traded punches proved ineffectual at this proximity. Knuckles grazed flesh but did little damage.

Then Rocky managed to wrap both hands around Lucky's throat, the maneuver taking him by surprise.

"You think you're special 'cause of your old man?" Rocky taunted. "You can die as easily as anyone else. And I'm the man to do it."

Unable to answer, Lucky struggled for air and saw black spots dancing in front of his eyes before he was able to break the other man's stranglehold on him. Gasping for breath and thinking to reconnoiter, he rolled away from Rocky and onto his knees, where he sucked in a lungful of air.

There was enough time for Rocky to get to his feet and kick out viciously.

Nearly blindsided, Lucky threw himself to his side, grabbing onto Rocky's boot before he could retract his leg. He twisted and jerked, gratified when the villain went down hard. Before Rocky could recover, Lucky was on him, grabbing the shirt at his neck and whipping his head so that it bounced off the hard earth a few times.

"That should knock some sense into you!" he muttered.

Rocky had nothing smart to say in return. Still, he wasn't finished. His fists latched on to Lucky's shirt, and his lower body bucked with inhuman strength.

An astonished Lucky went flying, feet over head, his body hurtling toward the edge of the cliff.

DISCRETION BEING the better part of valor, JoJo chose to forge ahead and let Paula come after her. Given the dangerous texture of the landscape, anything could happen. Should Paula drop the gun in the water a second time, she wouldn't so easily retrieve the weapon.

A worthy goal.

A last peek up at the helicopter shocked JoJo. High on the cliff overhead, a fight for dominance between two men ended with one of them nearly doing a dive feetfirst to the canyon floor. He caught himself on the flora wedged in the rock near the edge. His body slammed against the side of the cliff.

JoJo's eyes widened suddenly as she recognized him. "Lucky!" she screamed in terror.

What in the world was going on up there?

The man standing over him was Rocky Franzone.

A glance at Paula, whose attention, too, was riveted above for the moment, reminded JoJo to worry about herself. She couldn't help Lucky. She could only pray he wouldn't fall, and if he did, that he would survive.

Her back against the rocky wall, arms to her sides for balance, JoJo inched tentatively along the narrow ledge. Her heart pounded and her chest squeezed tight. If anything terrible happened to him because of her . . .

Lucky and Rocky and a helicopter!

Lucky must have figured out that Rocky was involved in her "accidents." Rocky must have been the help Paula talked about. He'd helped Paula spring Lester. He'd helped keep an eye on *her*. He'd provided an alibi for Paula the day Spitfire had conveniently disappeared. No doubt, he'd told Paula that she was going back to Rimrock to get her wallet, and Paula had ridden after her, hell-bent for leather, just waiting for her opportunity.

From the looks of it, Rocky must have been waiting for an opportunity to help Paula finish her off now.

Undoubtedly having guessed at the other man's duplicity, Lucky had come after him. But why alone, and where had he found a helicopter?

JoJo's heart ached. Lucky did care, whether or not he was willing to believe it himself, and now his life was in danger because of her. As she moved, she kept listening for some clue as to what was happening above the mechanical whir of the aircraft.

Then she heard a man's scream that made her heart stop.

And Paula's threat.

"You won't get away!" the other woman shouted. "I can't afford to let you show up back at the ranch. You won't leave this place alive."

But JoJo also heard the touch of panic threaded through the other woman's warning. Paula was afraid. JoJo didn't waste herself on a response. She needed every ounce of energy to get herself out of this mess, and the gorge was becoming even more harrowing. The cliffs on either side seemed to lean in toward each other and nearly touched at their tops. Below, the water grew deeper with each few steps she took. The bottom soon disappeared altogether.

Maybe Lucky had fallen into the creek. Please God, let him have landed in water. Though shallower than it was here, the water might have been enough to save his life. JoJo threw a glance over her shoulder the way she'd come but couldn't spot a man's body in or out of the water. The horses were spooked and dancing around each other.

Closer, her slight body stiff, Paula stood staring at the narrowing gorge as if reluctant to chance it. Her sound of frustration echoed along the stone walls, giving JoJo some measure of comfort. The less Paula liked the situation, the more vulnerable she'd be.

Observing the pool below her, JoJo realized this was trout heaven. Several foot-long fish swam along with her, as if they were curious about the strange creature above.

An odd thing to envision, considering the danger she was in.

And what might have happened to Lucky.

She bit the inside of her lip to distract herself. She couldn't think about it now. She couldn't cry. She didn't want to die.

The path narrowed and climbed as the gorge widened once more. The opposite cliffs were tiered with pine and oak that grew wherever the ground was level enough to provide a foothold for their roots. A several-yard drop below, the pool widened. And though the water was clear, JoJo could no longer see the bottom. In its midst, water beating against it, stood a lonely gravel bar.

A moment later, she tracked the narrow path around a bend and nearly stumbled into what could be a solution to her problem. A way to ambush Paula.

Backing into the shallow cave, JoJo looked around for some kind of weapon.

HEARING JOJO SCREAMING his name was almost the end of him. Lucky didn't give in to the temptation to look for her. Thank God. Rocky was upon him quickly enough. Fortunately, Lucky found a toehold in the rock face and anchored himself just in time.

"Now it's you who's whistling in the wind," the villain said with an evil grin. "Have a nice trip down!"

Rocky's foot came rushing at Lucky so fast, he barely had time to react—to let go with one hand. Once more, he grabbed on to the other man's boot, twisted and jerked.

Eyes wide in disbelief, Rocky took his turn at flying. The small of his back met the cliff edge, and the man screamed in agony, the sound bouncing off the sandstone walls. His arms flailed, hands shooting out, fingers scrabbling along the sparse growth.

A futile effort.

Rocky shot downward to meet his maker.

Lucky sagged against the prickly growth and waited for his heart to still before making a move. He suddenly felt weak, his limbs like rubber. He wasn't certain he could pull himself up to safety.

"Mr. Donatelli!" came a shout.

Lucky hadn't realized the chopper had landed. The pilot was kneeling near him and holding out a hand. Thankful, Lucky grabbed it and blessed the adrenaline he still had in reserve. A moment later, his feet were planted on blessed terra firma.

He chanced a glance down and saw an unconscious Rocky, sprawled on his back at the edge of the creek, both legs twisted at crazy angles.

"What now?" asked the pilot.

"Call in for help." Trying to breathe normally, Lucky was already going for the lariat that snaked across the sunbaked earth. "Tell the authorities that it's an emergency. We may have a dead man down there. Or if he's really luckless, he may still be alive."

"What about you, Mr. Donatelli? Don't you want to go back to the ranch?"

"Not yet." Not until he had the woman he loved safely in his arms, after which, he wouldn't ever let her go. Refusing to think JoJo might not live to hear his impassioned declaration of love, he quickly looped the lariat and threw it over his shoulder. "We have a lady to rescue. You can fly while you radio in, can't you?"

"Yes, sir!"

Together, they ran for the chopper.

HER ENTIRE BODY trembling, secluded in the shadows of what had turned out to be nothing more than a shallow cave, JoJo lay in wait for her pursuer. She'd found a few good-sized rocks and had stacked them before her. Her arsenal.

A nearby scrape alerted JoJo. Her hand fisted a stone. She heard Paula muttering to herself.

"C'mon. You *have* to do it. If you fail, you'll have a new address, all right, but not one that you'll like."

The other woman might have some misgivings, but JoJo suspected Paula's biggest regret was that she would have to do her dirty work herself and face-to-face. Previously, she'd tried to use circumstances—or Rocky Franzone—to her advantage. Now she had no choice but to look straight at her victim and pull the trigger. JoJo wondered if Paula really had the stomach for murder.

Not that she was holding her breath waiting for a last-minute change of heart, JoJo told herself.

The moment Paula stepped into view, JoJo acted, throwing the stone in her hand as hard as she could, her target the middle of the other woman's back.

With a screech, Paula stumbled and twirled, the gun waving frantically. "Where the hell are you, JoJo?"

In answer, JoJo let loose another missile, this one aimed at Paula's gun hand. She merely grazed the would-be killer, but the weapon fired, the bullet whining off the stone walls. Before Paula's eyes could adjust to the darkened interior of her shallow hiding place, JoJo attacked again, this rock bigger than the others.

Struck in the side, Paula took a step back...finding nothing but air below her free foot. Her eyes bugged out, and her mouth made a big *O* as she lost her balance. The gun discharged a second time, and a hysterical Paula tumbled backward into nothingness.

JoJo didn't wait for the splash. She crawled forward to see the other woman land in the creek. Relieved, she sat back on her haunches, wondering what came next. If she retraced her steps, no doubt Rocky would be waiting for her. But she had no clue as to what lay ahead. Besides which, she might never be able to climb up the rock face and get out of the gorge.

Mind whirling, she didn't immediately register the sounds from below. Paula. She focused on the woman thrashing and flailing at the water.

With a gurgle, Paula went under, then came up a few yards downstream, sputtering and coughing. She beat at the water as if her frenzied activity could overcome her obvious inability to swim. But under she went.

And JoJo knew a nonswimmer couldn't survive the creek, even with its gentle current. How ironic if Paula were to drown after leaving JoJo to do likewise in the flash flood.

Paula popped up farther downstream, her actions weaker, her frightened wail zinging down JoJo's spine.

JoJo got to her feet and, with a silent curse at her own stupidity, dived into the water. The pool was deep, its bottom dark with rotting leaves that had a slimy feel when she pushed herself up and toward Paula. A high school course in lifesaving would stand her in good stead, though why she was so concerned about the life of a woman who would see her dead, JoJo couldn't fathom.

And the drone of a helicopter in the distance warned her of oncoming danger.

Knowing that a panicked person could drown her rescuer, JoJo made certain she approached Paula directly from behind. She slipped an arm around the other woman's throat and lifted her face out of the water so she could breathe.

"Don't fight me!" JoJo ordered over the roar of the helicopter that was now in sight. "Relax and we'll both come out of this alive."

If Rocky didn't finish the job, she thought wryly.

There was no struggle left in Paula. She lay limp in the cradle of JoJo's arm. JoJo half allowed the current to take them downstream, half swam to maneuver them toward the approaching gravel bar. She wasn't certain if Paula was even conscious. When she could see the bottom rise into a slope, she lowered her feet and walked the rest of the way in. Once on the bank, she heaved Paula on her side and wondered if she would have to revive her.

Paula's eyes fluttered open, and she coughed out water.

And the helicopter hovered overhead.

No escape was in sight unless she tried to outswim the aircraft. Exhaustion precluded such activity—JoJo sank to the gravel bar to await her fate.

A flexible ladder shot out of the opening behind the pilot, and a man's legs followed, the booted feet finding purchase. JoJo squinted to watch, a certainty filling her. She'd recognize the way those jeans hugged that butt anywhere!

"Lucky!" she shouted. She shot to her feet as he shot down the ladder. A second later, she was enveloped in his arms, crying. "You're alive! You're alive."

"And so are you, thank God." Her face cradled in his hands, Lucky kissed her forehead, her nose, her chin. "I love you, JoJo Weston," he said fervently, commandeering her mouth before she could return the words.

JoJo sagged against Lucky and kissed him with all the adrenaline she had left, hoping against hope that they had a future after all.

LUCKY'S HIP WAS BURNING with knifelike pain by the time the chopper touched down. He helped a subdued Paula out of the aircraft. Then JoJo.

A county vehicle was parked in front of the house. Eli, Caroline, Vito, his father and two uniformed deputies rushed from the house. Hanging on to Paula's arm, Lucky limped toward them and met them halfway. Caroline threw herself against his chest.

"Are you all right?" she asked. "You look terrible."

"I'll be fine if you stop squeezing me so hard."

She stepped aside, and he came face-to-face with his father. Wearing his emotions, the old man looked as if he wanted to follow suit after Caroline. But Lucky knew Sally Donatelli was not a man who handled rejection easily, and so his father stood spine straight where he was.

"What the hell happened?" Sally demanded, tearing his gaze from Lucky to the women, who were almost dry but definitely bedraggled.

"A rat almost drowned," JoJo said.

Paula gave her a filthy look, JoJo's reward for saving her hide. Lucky wasn't so certain he would have been as generous.

"The rescue chopper is at the canyon," Lucky said. "We got word that Rocky's still alive. He and this *lady* were hand in hand in trying to kill JoJo." He pushed her toward the deputies. "She's all yours, guys."

One of the cops read Paula her rights. Seeming resigned to her fate, she temporarily waived her right to an attorney, admitted that she'd been the one to shoot Adair the evening before, that her last name was Carbury rather than Gibson and that she'd hired Rocky to help her eliminate JoJo before leaving the East coast.

They'd taken turns following JoJo around Las Vegas. And from day one, Paula had planned on leaving poor Lester with the blame for JoJo's death.

While she was giving one man details, the other deputy suggested they go inside. After Lucky and JoJo gave statements, the deputies left with a handcuffed Paula.

"Well, all's well that ends well," JoJo said.

His father locked gazes with Lucky. "You need anything at all, you ask."

Lucky knew Sally was leaving a door open with the statement. Part of him wanted to throw the offer back into his father's face. Part of him wanted to thank the old man. He nodded and said, "I'll keep that in mind." He needed time to sort out his feelings. Somewhere, he'd lost the rage that used to fuel him.

Sally rose. "Caroline, you ready to leave?"

"Yes, Papa. My bags are in the car."

"Your sister's coming with me. Vito's gonna drive her car back to Vegas."

Lucky was amazed that his sister didn't insist on staying with him, fussing over him. He figured his father had something to do with that. A reason to be grateful, whether he wanted to be or not.

"Caroline." Lucky gave her a quick hug. "I'm sure I'll be seeing you."

"Damn straight," she muttered.

His father first looked expectant, then disappointed when Lucky extended him no like offer. "We'd better go." He stared at Lucky. "Unless there's some reason for us to stay…"

"No, we'll be fine."

Only after they'd climbed in the chopper did Lucky feel regret and a renewed sense of loss.

But JoJo was there, her arm wrapped around his waist, her head on his shoulder, and Lucky told himself she was all he needed.

"I DON'T WANT you to leave."

With a happy smile, JoJo sprawled in the passenger seat of Lucky's Bronco as they drove along the bumpy ridge above the canyon to recover her Cherokee. "Say it again."

"You've already made me say it at least a dozen times since yesterday," Lucky complained.

Several times during the night, while they'd held each other, too tired and sore to do anything more physical.

"Well . . . I might actually be starting to believe it."

He lifted her hand and kissed the fingers tenderly. "I love you and I don't want you to leave."

"What *do* you want?"

"Are you deaf?"

"I mean if I stay—" her pulse thrummed "—where do we go from here?"

"Anywhere you want."

What JoJo wanted was a more definite idea of how *he* saw their future together. What she said was, "You mean you'd leave the ranch?" She couldn't help teasing him just a bit.

"JoJo, you know my plans for the place." He glanced at her, brow furrowing. "Surely, you can't be asking me to go back to Las Vegas."

"I think you should."

"Does it mean that much to you?" he asked, clearly torn between pleasing her and his own demons.

"I don't mean permanently," JoJo assured him. "A visit. To heal the breach between you and your father. You both wanted to. I could tell."

Silent, Lucky seemed to be thinking about it.

And JoJo thought about his heroic rescue of her the day before. She'd been so relieved to find him unhurt but for some cuts and bruises...and his limp was a bit more pronounced than normal. Truth to tell, she was having trouble moving normally herself. But they were both well-off compared to Rocky. Two broken legs, a broken arm and shoulder, several broken ribs and some internal damage.

"You were right about my running away from the situation," Lucky finally admitted. "You've been right about a lot of things."

"And don't forget it," she warned him smartly. "How *did* you feel when you saw Sally?"

"Mixed. Part of me wanted to punch him out. Part of me wanted to throw my arms around him."

"But you didn't do either."

"Sometimes I have problems expressing how I feel."

"Really?" she asked in an exaggerated tone.

Though he'd had no problem convincing JoJo he loved her. Now, what to do about it. She didn't care if she never returned to Las Vegas—at least not permanently.

"If I stay," she said, "I want to be partners with you in every sense of the word."

"Are you saying you'll marry me?"

"You haven't asked."

Lucky stomped on the brakes, making the Bronco buck. He cut the engine and threw open his door. Before she could react, he'd raced around to her side and was pulling her out of the passenger seat.

"I guess I have a hell of a time making myself clear," Lucky said with the devilish grin she'd grown to love. "I wouldn't have asked you to stay if I didn't intend to make an honest woman of you."

Heart soaring, JoJo feigned indignation. "Honest?"

"Don't go getting your dander up. Will you marry me?"

What an unforgettable spot for a proposal! Blue sky, red rock, green juniper. What more could a woman ask for? A lot, JoJo thought, wondering how he was going to take *her* proposal.

She took a big breath. "And we'll be partners, right?"

Lucky gazed at her suspiciously. "Define your terms."

"The business. You have the land, but you need capital. I have money, and I need a good investment."

"That's sweet of you, JoJo, but a nest egg isn't going to go far in the scheme of things."

"What about an inheritance?"

"How big an inheritance?"

"I don't quite know yet, but I'd guess it'd be substantial enough to get started on those plans of yours." She bit the inside of her mouth waiting for his response.

"Oliver Phipps?" he asked.

She nodded.

He shook his head. "I don't know. Another man's money—"

"Oliver wanted me to be happy. He'd be thrilled to know I found someone I really and truly loved."

"A man has his pride."

"Pride can make a man lonely." She touched Lucky's face. "Haven't you been lonely long enough, Lucky? I have. The money doesn't mean anything to me if I don't have you."

He caved in right before her eyes. "I really am a lucky devil. Partner." And kissed her to seal the bargain.

Epilogue

"I thought this was supposed to be a family gathering," Sasha griped as Lucky climbed on top of the new bucking chute.

"I told you my husband wanted to show off a little," JoJo said, unable to hide her pride. "Now that things around here are on a roll."

New guest quarters were in progress, and a new barn was up, as was this corral for the Friday-night rodeos. Lucky had been teaching the wranglers a trick or two. So far, the family had watched some bareback-riding and calf-roping demonstrations. Lucky was going to give them the big finish.

"I'm hungry," Sasha complained.

"My wife isn't known for her patience," Nick said, hugging Sasha's growing body to him.

The honeymoon had been quite successful, JoJo thought, in that Nick and Sasha were expecting. She grinned at her best friend and received a warm, happy smile in return.

Wearing baggy pants and a fright wig, his face painted like a clown's, Eli took his place in the center of the new corral with another of the similarly groomed wranglers. And a Brahma bull was released from a holding pen into the bucking chute.

"I think Lucky's going to try to get himself killed," announced Caroline, the voice of doom.

JoJo gave her a wicked look. "My husband is not suicidal."

While she and Caroline shared no love for one another, they had come to terms. Peace reigned among all three Donatelli women, thank goodness. Caroline hadn't even objected at Lucky's plans for the ranch, not even when she learned JoJo was financing the expansion. JoJo also planned on using her show-business experience to produce and star in a Saturday-night show.

"Couldn't prove it by me," Sally grumbled, though he watched with interest as Lucky gingerly straddled the bull's back. "Any man who purposely crosses a bull has a death wish."

Remembering her own encounter with him, JoJo said, "Old Bushwhacker isn't all that deadly."

But the moment the chute opened, her heart was in her throat. Nearly two thousand pounds of angry bull did his best to unseat Lucky. His gloved hand wrapped in a flat, plaited rope, he hung on, his body moving with the bull. Bushwhacker dodged one way, then the other, bucking like crazy, after which he turned in a tight circle. All the while Eli and the other wrangler-cum-rodeo-clown danced around the livid animal, waiting for their chance at the action.

Time was up, and Lucky jumped off the bull's back, somehow managing to stay on his feet. The breath caught in JoJo's throat as Bushwhacker went after him, but the clowns created a diversion and drove the animal through another gate as Lucky hopped up on the split-rail fence and threw his legs over.

His grin devilish, he jumped down and asked, "So what do you think?"

The Donatellis all circled him.

"I think you're insane!" Caroline said, protective as always.

Nick held out his hand for Lucky to shake. "Good show," he said, pulling Lucky into his arms for a brotherly hug.

"I'm proud of you, son."

Lucky and Sally stared at each other for a moment. And JoJo's eyes filled with tears when the two men wrapped their arms around each other. Lucky drew back, pulled her to his side, his other arm still around his father. JoJo smiled up at Lucky, knowing he was finally free of the past.

NO SIN TOO GREAT
Jasmine Cresswell

She'll do anything…

Lie, cheat, steal—Caroline Hogarth will do anything to get her three-year-old son back.

Her father-in-law will do anything to prevent it. Anything. Which may explain why Caroline wakes up in bed with a dead man.

Or why the headlines shout: Captain of Industry Dies in Mistress's Bed…

Publicly labelled a whore and an unfit mother, Caroline needs help and she needs it fast—but there's no one in Chicago her father-in-law can't buy. Except, maybe, Jack Fletcher—a man Caroline is prepared to seduce, if necessary.

So what if he's a convicted murderer? So what if he doesn't trust her?

So what if he's a priest?

NO SIN TOO GREAT IS A SIZZLING NEW NOVEL FROM THE BESTSELLING AUTHOR OF *DESIRES AND DECEPTIONS*.

MIRA®

▼™ SILHOUETTE
Intrigue™

COMING NEXT MONTH

BABY VS. THE BAR   M.J. Rodgers

Justice Inc.

Attorney Marc Truesdale was prepared to pull out all the stops
to protect the interests of his cute eighteen-month-old client.
But the confirmed bachelor was *not* prepared to fall for the
little boy or his contrary mother. Nor was he prepared to enter
a courtroom where conspiracy was the name of the game…

RECKLESS LOVER   Carly Bishop

Dangerous Men

Even the Witness Protection programme couldn't hide Eden
Kelley. When a dark and dangerous stranger blasted into her
hideaway, she was imprisoned as much by the sorcery in his
eyes as by the strength of his arms. But who was this man, and
what did he want from her?

EXPOSÉ   Saranne Dawson

Like a flash, wonderboy reporter Sam Winters stormed back
into Kate Stevens' life—and under the conjugal roof. But Kate
was on to the biggest story of her career, and someone wanted
her dead! Sam claimed he'd protect her, but Kate knew he
would do anything for a story. Could his open arms and deep
blue eyes be telling the truth this time?

MIDNIGHT COWBOY   Adrianne Lee

Her Protector

For years, Jack Starett had been hunting her down—but all
Andrea Hart knew about *him* was that he was the most
powerfully attractive man she'd ever met. But something in
Jack's melancholy eyes warned of danger, something in his
heated kisses almost frightened her. Andrea needed someone
to watch over her, but was her midnight cowboy a white
knight—or a threat to her safety?

COMING NEXT MONTH FROM

SILHOUETTE®

Sensation

A thrilling mix of passion, adventure and drama

UNCERTAIN ANGELS Kim Cates
ONE GOOD MAN Kathleen Creighton
CUTS BOTH WAYS Dee Holmes
SERIOUS RISKS Rachel Lee

Special Edition

Satisfying romances packed with emotion

PART-TIME WIFE Susan Mallery
THE REBEL'S BRIDE Christine Flynn
MARRIAGE-TO-BE? Gail Link
WAITING AT THE ALTAR Amy Frazier
RESIST ME IF YOU CAN Janis Reams Hudson
LONESOME COWBOY Lois Faye Dyer

Desire

Provocative, sensual love stories for the woman of today

THE ACCIDENTAL BODYGUARD Ann Major
HARDEN Diana Palmer
FATHER OF THE BROOD Elizabeth Bevarly
THE GROOM, I PRESUME? Annette Broadrick
THE PRODIGAL GROOM Karen Leabo
FALCON'S LAIR Sara Orwig

To celebrate the **1000**th Desire™ title we're giving away a year's supply of Silhouette Desire® novels — absolutely *FREE!*

All you have to do is complete the puzzle below and send it to us by 31 December 1996.

The first 10 correct entries drawn from the bag will each win 12 month's free supply of seductive and breathtaking Silhouette Desire books (6 books every month—worth over £160). The second correct 10 entries drawn will each win a Silhouette music cassette.

S
E
N
S
U
O
U
S

Word	Letters
SENSUOUS	8
DESIRE	6
DARING	6
SEDUCTIVE	9
EMOTIONAL	9
COMPELLING	10
PASSIONATE	10
CAPTIVATING	11
ADVENTUROUS	11
PROVOCATIVE	11

Please turn over for entry details

CELEBRATION 1000

How to enter

There are ten words listed overleaf, each of which fits into spaces in the grid according to their length. All you have to do is fit the correct word into the appropriate spaces that have been provided for its letters. We've even done the first one for you!

When you have completed the grid, don't forget to fill in your name and address in the space provided below and pop this page into an envelope (you don't even need a stamp) and post it today. Hurry—competition ends 31st December 1996.

Silhouette® Words of Love
FREEPOST
Croydon
Surrey
CR9 3WZ

Are you a Reader Service Subscriber?　　　Yes ❏　　　No ❏

Ms/Mrs/Miss/Mr　_____

Address　_____

_____

_____ Postcode _____

One application per household.

mps MAILING PREFERENCE SERVICE　　DMA　　SILC96